"GET A CLUE, DAD!"

Dad looked at me closely. "Have you been talking to Iris behind our backs?"

"What if I have? So what?"

"Sara, listen," Dad said. "It's natural to feel sorry for Iris and want to help her. But becoming friends with her is not the way to do it."

I had to laugh. "Get a clue, Dad," I said. "I don't feel sorry for Iris. I envy her."

FRANCESS LANTZ grew up in Bucks County, Pennsylvania, dreaming of becoming a writer and an artist. Inspired by the Beatles, she turned to writing and performing music, but a job as a children's librarian brought her back to her writing career.

Ms. Lantz now lives in Santa Barbara, California, with her husband and her son.

SOMEONE TO LOVE

Francess Lantz

AN AVON FLARE BOOK

AVON BOOKS, INC.
1350 Avenue of the Americas
New York, New York 10019

Copyright © 1997 by Francess Lantz
Published by arrangement with the author
Visit our website at http://www.AvonBooks.com
Library of Congress Catalog Card Number: 96-31434
ISBN: 0-380-77590-5

First Avon Flare Printing: February 1998
First Avon Hardcover Printing: February 1997

AVON FLARE TRADEMARK REG. U.S. PAT. OFF. AND IN OTHER COUNTRIES, MARCA REGISTRADA, HECHO EN U.S.A.

Printed in the U.S.A.

WCD 10 9 8 7 6 5 4 3 2

For Preston

With thanks to John M. Landsberg, M.D., Ellen Jackson,
Lou Lynda Richards, Mary Smith, Rebecca Martin,
Megan Schlueter, and Janice Sanders, L.C.S.W.,
California Department of Social Services

September 20

DEAR MYSTERY BABY,

I suppose it all started the Friday I got suspended from school. It was BLT day at the cafeteria and Marc, Lauren, Forest, Noah, and I were staging a protest demonstration. We're all vegetarians and members of PETA—People for the Ethical Treatment of Animals—so naturally, we're not exactly enthusiastic about eating dead pig flesh on toast.

Still, staging a protest was a big move for us. Last year we probably would have bought the sandwiches and removed the bacon, or maybe brought something from home. But over the summer Marc went to a bunch of PETA meetings down in Los Angeles, and now he says it isn't enough simply to avoid meat and refuse to wear leather shoes. If we want to change the world, we have to get out there and change people's minds. And the best way to do that is to make a scene.

So that's exactly what we did. The five of us put on rubber pig noses and carried signs that said, "Love Animals. Don't Eat Them." Then we marched past the lunch line and through the cafeteria, oinking loudly.

Laguna Verde High isn't exactly what you'd call a hotbed of militant protest. When kids get upset about something, they usually write a letter to the school board, or maybe collect signatures on a petition. Which is why our little parade really made people sit up and take notice. Kids stared, teachers frowned, cafeteria ladies gasped. Even the cooks came out of the kitchen to see what was going on.

I could feel my cheeks turning red. I'm not the type of person who likes to have people stare at me. But if you don't stand up for what you believe in, what's the point of believing in it at all? Besides, Marc didn't look embarrassed. Neither did Noah, Lauren, or Forest.

Then Jake Halsey, well-known football star and congenital idiot, stood up and shouted, "Put an apple in Forest's mouth and she'd be the spitting image of a prize porker!" That was a reference to the fact that Forest is slightly chubby, unlike the anorexic cheerleaders that Jake Halsey goes for.

There were a few laughs and a lot of snickers. Now Forest did look embarrassed. But Noah shot Jake a dirty look and said, "With or without an apple, you're the spitting image of an ass." The cafeteria broke up.

That's Noah for you. He's like the Bomb Squad, always ready to diffuse a tense moment with a joke or a clever put-down. I wish I could do that. When I'm upset I usually get more and more uptight and serious until everyone around me wants to shake me and shout, "Lighten up!"

"All right, that's enough," a deep voice said. I turned to see Mr. Ferris, math teacher and cafeteria monitor, walking toward us. "You've made your point, kids. Now take a seat and let's get on with lunch."

I was going to do it, but Marc had other ideas. He knew the entire school was staring at us, waiting to find out what we were going to do next. We would have been fools not to take advantage of it. So he jumped up on an empty table and announced, "Studies have shown that pigs are smarter than dogs."

Lauren climbed up beside him. "Pigs are gentle, loyal, and they make great pets," she said.

"Would you eat a PLT—a puppy, lettuce, and tomato sandwich?" Noah asked. A disgusted groan went up from the crowd.

Marc motioned for Noah, Forest, and me to climb up on the table. I followed them up and looked around. Everyone was watching us. I felt scared, but powerful, too.

"Why do you think it's gross to fry up a dog and eat it, but perfectly normal to do the same thing to a pig?" Marc demanded.

"It just doesn't make sense," I piped up. "They're both living things."

"Okay, time out," Mr. Ferris broke in. "I want you kids off the table right now. This is a cafeteria, not a barnyard."

"What's wrong with a barnyard?" Marc asked. "If you want to see real dirt, filth, and horror, you should visit a slaughterhouse."

Suddenly I had an inspiration. It wasn't part of our plan, but then neither was climbing on the table and talking about puppyburgers. Besides, I had a feeling that Marc would approve.

I opened my backpack and pulled out my cassette

player. In it was a tape Marc had brought back from a PETA meeting. I hit the play button. Instantly, the cafeteria was filled with the frightened squeals of pigs being slaughtered. My fellow students listened, their eyes widening as they slowly began to realize what they were hearing.

"Sara Dewherst, turn that thing off!" Mr. Ferris shouted. "Young lady, you and your friends are in serious trouble."

But I already knew that because the school principal, Ms. Saldano, was standing in the cafeteria doorway giving me the evil eye. I turned off the cassette deck and climbed down from the table. I didn't want to care, but I did. I guess after a lifetime of being a good girl, it just comes naturally.

Only Marc looked calm. He turned and smiled at me, and suddenly Ms. Saldano and her evil eye didn't seem so important. I smiled back.

"Love animals. Don't eat them," Marc said with quiet conviction as he walked toward the door. I hugged the cassette player to my chest and followed.

Okay, Mystery Baby, you're probably wondering what all this has to do with you. Well, it's like this: my mother's friend Janie told me she kept a journal when she and Bob were adopting their son, and it really helped her sort out her emotions. Plus, she plans to pass the journal on to Kenya someday so he'll know where he came from. Janie told Mom and Dad they should keep a journal about adopting you, but last year they barely got it together to write Christmas cards.

Lucky for them, they've got a writer in the family— at least that's what my English teachers are always telling me. Personally, I'm not so sure. Putting words together is easy for me, but does that make me a writer? And is that what I want to be? I don't know. But I do know that you deserve to hear the true story of where you came from. Listen . . .

Twenty minutes later, I was riding down Cliff Drive with my mother. "What in God's name were you thinking of?" she demanded.

"I think that's pretty obvious," I said. "I was trying to make a point about something I feel very strongly about."

"And you got yourself suspended in the process."

I rolled my eyes. "Come on, Mom. We didn't do anything that bad. Marc says Ms. Saldano is just trying to make an example of us so no one else will dare to stage a protest at school."

"A three-day suspension," Mom went on, ignoring me. "That's going to look just great on your permanent record."

That was meant to scare me, and it did, a little. But I wasn't going to let it show. "Maybe we should just tattoo it on my chest," I said. "Kind of like *The Scarlet Letter*, only instead of an A, it'll be a big red S. Then you can lead me through the town square and let everyone throw stones."

"This isn't a joke," Mom said. "If you want to be a vegetarian, fine. That's your choice. But forcing your views on others—especially in such a tasteless manner—is completely inappropriate."

"Oh, you mean like dressing up as the Grim Reaper to protest the Vietnam War, for example? Wow, that is in bad taste." I was referring to a photograph I'd discovered in one of my parents' photo albums. It showed Mom and Dad, both eighteen, marching in an antiwar demonstration. Dad was dressed as the Grim Reaper and he had all his hair. Mom was wearing army fatigues and she was practically skinny.

"I'm beginning to wish I'd burned that photo," Mom said with an exasperated sigh. "Listen Sara, you're not the first teenager who's wanted to save the world. It's a normal feeling, a necessary feeling. But my job as your parent is to remind you not to let your passions overwhelm your good sense."

I stared out the window. The way Mom talked, I felt like a specimen in a laboratory. Typical American Teenager Experiencing Emotion Number 432, the label read. But is wanting to save the world just a phase I'm going through? Am I going to grow up and turn into Mom and Dad, always looking out for Number One? I just can't believe it. There has to be another way. There just has to be.

Mom, however, seems determined to stop me from finding it. "You know, Sara," she said, "suspension isn't a vacation. I expect you to help out at the restaurant the next couple of days."

I leaned my head against the side window and let out a groan. Talk about a jail sentence. Mom and Dad own a restaurant on the beach called The Wharf. The specialties of the house? Seafood and prime rib.

"Sara, get a move on," my father called as he backed through the swinging doors that led to the kitchen. "There's a party of four waiting for you to clear table fifteen."

"Okay, okay. Just give me a second," I said. "I didn't get any lunch, you know."

"Whose fault is that?"

I ignored him. "Alvino made me a zucchini chimichanga," I said. I took a bite. It was delicious. "You should add this to the menu."

"Honey, the people who eat lunch here don't want chimichangas. This is a steak and seafood restaurant."

"Whose fault is that?" I mimicked.

"Don't be smart." He turned to Alvino and pushed two plates under the hot lamp. "Give the prime rib another thirty seconds, wouldya? And put some new fries on the other plate. The lady says they're cold."

Alvino nodded. "Yes, sir."

I rolled my eyes. When my father speaks, his employees jump. Of course, they have to. He's the boss, the owner, not to mention a white guy. They're Mexican-American and poor. I wonder what they say about him when his back is turned.

I scarfed down the rest of the chimichanga and left the kitchen. The restaurant was bustling with the usual crowd—middle-aged and elderly white people, the type who drive Cadillacs, smoke cigarettes, and subsist on a diet of martinis, iceberg lettuce, and red meat. They glanced disapprovingly at me as I cleared table fifteen. I think my babydoll dress and purple high-tops shocked them. At least, I hope so.

Dad breezed by, smiling. "Did you finish your chimichanga?"

I knew he was trying to make up. I smiled back. "Yeah. Thanks."

"Good crowd today."

Dad wanted me to be interested in the restaurant,

and I was—only not in the way he hoped. All I could think about was the photograph on the wall by the rest rooms—the one that shows The Wharf the way it used to look when my parents first bought it. Back then it was a cool little beach shack, frequented by surfers and fishermen. Now its official title is Wharf Enterprises, Inc., and my parents are thinking of starting a chain of Wharf clones up and down the coast.

"I think you should give Alvino a raise," I said.

Dad frowned. "He gets the same as or more than every other chef in town working at a restaurant of comparable size."

"So for once don't do what everyone else is doing," I suggested. "Follow your heart."

"My heart tells me you'll be going to college in a couple of years, and that means I have to come up with some big bucks. I wish someone would give *me* a raise."

A typical Dad response—sidestepping the issue by changing the subject to something he feels comfortable discussing, like how hard he works or how much trouble I cause him. I was all set to tell him that when my mom stepped up behind us. Her eyes were shining and she looked excited.

"Marty," she said, "guess who's here? Janie and Bob."

Dad broke into a grin. "No kidding? I haven't seen them since they got back from their trip."

Janie and Bob have been friends with my parents since their hippie days. Only unlike my folks, they haven't settled down and gone to sleep. Bob teaches art at the local junior college, and Janie makes pottery. Every couple of years Bob takes time off and they go on some totally thrilling adventure. Two years ago, they trekked across India. This year they went island-hopping in the South Pacific.

"And get this," my mother announced. "They have a baby with them."

I looked over my mom's shoulder. Janie and Bob were sitting at a table near the window. Their menus were open, but instead of looking at them, they were making goo-goo faces at the baby in Bob's lap. I looked closer. Janie and Bob are both blond and fair, but this baby had light brown skin and dark, fuzzy hair.

Mom and Dad headed over to talk to them. I finished clearing the table and hurried after them. I got there just in time to hear Janie say, "Meet Kenya Thomas McDermott. He's three weeks old today."

"Hi, Kenya," Dad said, reaching down to pat his downy head. The baby cooed. "Whose kid?" he asked.

"Ours," she replied with a grin.

Mom looked puzzled. "You weren't pregnant when you left for your trip. So what . . . I mean, how—?"

Janie laughed. "Kenya is adopted."

"No kidding?" Dad said. "Gosh, I saw something on TV that said most agencies won't accept couples over forty. How'd you manage it?"

"We didn't go through an agency," Bob explained. "It was an open adoption."

"You mean you met the mother?" Mom asked, looking a little startled.

"The birthmother," Janie corrected. "Yes, we met her. In fact, we were at Kenya's birth."

"His birthmother is white and his birthfather is half-black and half-Filipino," Bob said. "It's a good combination, don't you think?"

Dad looked down at Kenya. "He's gorgeous, that's for sure."

They went on talking about the baby, but I wasn't listening. I was thinking about how cool Janie and Bob are. They're artists, they travel the globe, and now they're the parents of an adopted baby—a baby of color, no less.

I tried to imagine Mom and Dad doing something like that, but I couldn't. No way would they shake up their ordered little lives by adopting a kid. Besides, I figured they were too busy hanging on to their personal piece of the American dream to share it with anyone else.

A group of four white-haired women walked through the door. "Oops, gotta go," Dad said, putting on his cheery restaurant face as he hurried over to greet them.

"We'd love to have you over for dinner," Mom said to Janie and Bob. "I'll call you, okay?" She turned to me. "Sara, clear those tables in the back please. It's time for the one o'clock crowd to show up."

"Yeah, yeah," I muttered. I walked off, thinking how amazing and weird and scary and thrilling it would be to adopt a baby, but figuring it was about as likely that lightning would strike the restaurant and turn the four white-haired women into life-sized roasted marshmallows.

Little did I know I'd soon be meeting your birthmother—and you.

September 24

It was Friday evening, three days after the infamous Laguna Verde High School BLT protest. I had spent the entire time bussing tables at The Wharf and catching up on missed homework, and believe me, I was ready to scream. Clearly, it was time to get away from Mom and Dad and get crazy. So I called Lauren.

"Congratulate me," I said when I heard her voice. "I survived three days of slave labor."

"At least you were around people," she said. "I spent the whole time stuck in this stupid house, watching daytime television. My brain has turned to oatmeal."

"Do you think anyone missed us?" I asked. "What did Trish say?" Trish is Lauren's big sister. She's a year ahead of us at school.

"The usual," she replied. "Some people think we're jerks, a few were impressed. Most kids were just happy for a little lunchtime entertainment. But Ms. Steiner used the whole thing to start a class discussion about nonviolent protest and passive resistance."

"Cool. So let's celebrate. What are you doing tonight?"

"*Nada.* You want to go downtown, maybe eat something and see a movie?"

"Sure." I put my hand over the receiver and shouted, "Mom? Dad? Can you drive me downtown?"

"No can do," my mother called back from the other end of the house. "Janie and Bob are coming over with the new baby."

Can you believe it? Nobody tells me anything around here. I put the phone to my ear and told Lauren about Janie and Bob. "I want to hang around and hear how they found their baby, okay?"

"Sure, dump me for a drooling infant. See if I care. Maybe you can meet me later at Espresso Loco."

I hung up and walked into the kitchen. Mom was spooning stuffing between the pork chops. "Cook some of that stuffing separately, will you?" I asked. "I've decided to stay home."

"I only made enough for the chops," she answered. "You'll have to cook yourself a veggie burger."

I frowned. I've been a vegetarian for over six months and Mom still refuses to alter her cooking one bit to accommodate me. "Just eat the rice and vegetables and leave the meat," she says, even though I've told her a thousand times I need rice and beans to have complete protein. I think she figures that eventually I'll see that meat sitting on the plate and become overwhelmed with carnivorous desire. Yeah, right. I'm a human being, Mom, not a wolf.

"As long as you're joining us, how about helping out?" Mom said. "Set the table."

I was putting down the wineglasses when Janie and

Bob showed up. Janie was carrying Kenya in a sling around her shoulder. He was fast asleep and making little sucking noises.

"Hey, hey, hey," Dad said, walking in from the living room, "the happy family has arrived."

"Hi, folks," Bob said. "Hi, Sara, How's life?"

Janie and Bob have got to be the only friends of my parents who don't ask me what grade I'm in and how I'm doing at school. I love them for it. "Okay. How was your trip?"

"Cosmic," he replied. "In fact, almost as cosmic as parenthood."

"Don't believe anything he says," Janie said. "He's not thinking straight. Sleep deprivation, you know."

"This kid wants to eat every three hours, day and night," Bob said. "I think he's going to be a linebacker."

Dad laughed. "Don't expect any sympathy from me. Sara had colic the first six months of her life. The only way we could get her to sleep was to run the vacuum cleaner."

"I read about that," Janie said. "Apparently, the noise creates sensory overload and the baby falls asleep as an escape."

"That's sick," I said.

"Hey, we were desperate," Dad replied. "Anyway, it was good practice for you. Today you can play your Walkman at full volume without even wincing."

Everyone laughed except me. Dad thinks he can make fun of me because I'm not an adult, and therefore my lifestyle isn't to be taken seriously. But watch out if I try to tease him. Then he says I'm being disrespectful.

Mom bustled in with the food. Bob took Kenya out

13

of his sling and put him in one of those carseat/cradle contraptions. He set it on the end of the table and we all sat down.

"Look at him," Mom sighed, gazing at Kenya. "He's perfection."

"Tell us how you decided to adopt," Dad said.

Bob took a pork chop and a helping of rice. "It's hard to explain, really. When we got home from the South Pacific we felt . . . well, empty somehow. The whole routine—making our art, teaching, taking care of the house—I was surprised to find it didn't seem like enough anymore."

"It was me, really," Janie said. "I'd always been certain I didn't want children. But on our trip I found myself staring at babies, even asking strangers if I could hold their child. It was crazy. I mean, I'm forty-five years old. I thought my biological clock had stopped ticking."

"So we talked it over and decided we were too old—"

"And too chicken," Janie added with a chuckle.

"To go through the whole pregnancy thing."

"That's when we started thinking about adoption," Janie said, reaching for the peas. "Why add to the population problem? There are so many unwanted kids in the world that need parents."

"We were thinking of international adoption, or maybe an older kid who was stuck in the foster care system," Bob explained. "But then a friend who teaches in a high school over in Ellwood told me about Megan. She was in one of his classes. He knew she was pregnant and uncertain about keeping the baby."

It floored me to hear that the birthmother is still in high school. I mean, she can't be much older than me. "What's she like?" I asked. "Kenya's birthmother, I mean."

"She's seventeen," Janie said. "Gentle and shy. She wants to be a veterinary assistant."

Bob pulled out his wallet. "We have a photo of her. Do you want to see it?"

I took the photo. It looked like a high school yearbook shot. Megan was small with high cheekbones and long, black hair. She was wearing a silver necklace like the ones they sell at the weekend craft show at the beach. I'd almost bought one just like it.

I found myself wondering what it would be like to be in Megan's shoes. I would completely freak. Not that I've ever actually done anything to get myself pregnant, but I came pretty close with Marc last summer. I mean, what if his parents hadn't come home that evening and we'd actually gone all the way? I could have ended up like Megan.

"Wasn't it strange meeting the mother—birthmother—of your child?" Mom asked.

"Yes, at first," Janie admitted. "You feel like you want something from this young woman you aren't supposed to have. Like you're using her. But that feeling disappears when you realize you're all in it together, doing what's best for the baby."

"It was hard sometimes," Bob said with a nod, "but I'm glad we got to know her. We've agreed to communicate twice a year. We want Kenya to know where he comes from. Besides, he might want to get in touch with her someday."

"You could handle that?" Mom asked, raising her eyebrows.

Janie nodded. "I think so. I hope so, for Kenya's

sake. He's going to figure out pretty quickly he doesn't look like us. I think he deserves to know where he got that great hair."

"What about his birthfather?" Dad asked.

"We never met him," Bob replied. "Apparently, he had no interest in becoming involved. Megan got him to sign the papers and that was that."

Kenya woke up and began to whimper. "Decided to join in the conversation, eh?" Bob said with a grin. He unstrapped the baby from his seat and picked him up. "Come here, big guy."

"Can I hold him?" Mom asked.

"Of course," he said, handing Kenya across the table. "Here, kiddo, go to Aunt Jeanette."

Mom held Kenya as if he were a piece of antique china that might shatter at any moment. "I'm out of practice," she laughed. Janie handed Dad a bottle and he held it to the baby's lips. Kenya began to suck happily.

"Whew, I'm having déjà vu," Dad said. "Remember when we first brought Sara home from the hospital?"

"We were living in that awful studio apartment near Butterfly Beach," Mom reminisced. "We had no money and absolutely no idea what we were doing." She laughed and shook her head. "Back then, we thought love was all you needed to get by."

Dad snorted through his nose. "We learned differently pretty fast. When you have a baby in the house, your priorities change."

"What do you mean?" I asked.

"I was playing in a band, making about a hundred bucks a week. Your mother was working as a waitress at the original Wharf, but she quit when we had you.

We were so broke. You didn't even have a crib for the first month. You slept on a mattress on the floor with us."

"So? What's wrong with that?" I asked.

"We could barely afford diapers," Dad said. "You can't raise a child like that. It isn't right. So I quit the band and got a job washing dishes at the Wharf. A few years later, I owned the place," he added proudly.

But I couldn't see why that was something to be proud of. If you ask me, Dad should have kept on with his music. I've heard him play his guitar along with the radio, late at night when he thinks I'm asleep. He's got talent. Maybe if he'd stuck with it, he could have become famous.

I closed my eyes and imagined myself as a little kid, dancing joyfully in the grass as my father performed at an outdoor concert in front of thousands of people. Now that would be a great way to spend a childhood!

Mom's voice broke into my fantasy. "If we were raising a baby now, things would be different," she said wistfully. "We'd have more money, more experience . . ."

"Yeah, but don't forget," Dad warned, glancing at me as he sipped his wine, "babies grow up and turn into teenagers who blame their parents for everything."

Everyone laughed except me. I don't blame my mother and father for everything. Actually, I wouldn't be surprised if deep down they blame me for coming along and putting an end to their loose, laid-back lives. I mean, they say they're glad they left it all behind, but come on—don't they ever want to blow off their responsibilities and just go wild?

And then I had a startling thought. Maybe, just maybe, I was an accident. An unplanned mistake. And maybe the real reason Mom and Dad said they didn't miss their old lives was because they didn't want me to find out that they were a lot happier before I came along.

I glanced over at Kenya. Everyone was watching him, oohing and ahhing over his every burp and gurgle. Suddenly, I felt I had to get out of there. I pushed back my chair and stood up.

"I'm going to catch the bus and meet Lauren at Espresso Loco," I said. "I'll be back by ten."

"Sara, wait," Mom called. "You didn't even finish your veggie burger." But I was already out the door.

"Teenagers," I heard Dad grumble as the door slammed behind me.

October 27

Hi, little embryo. Let me tell you, it feels pretty weird writing to someone who doesn't even exist yet. Well, I guess that isn't totally accurate. You do exist. According to Janie and Bob, you've been living and growing inside your birthmother for almost six months now. It's just that you haven't been born yet, and according to the book I checked out of the library, you look kind of like that creature who burst out of the guy's stomach in the movie *Alien,* only without the teeth.

Okay, okay, so maybe I'm exaggerating a little. I usually do. My father says that's because when you lead with your emotions, your brain strikes out. But how can you claim to be truly alive unless you feel things passionately? I mean, look at Dad. His idea of intense emotion is shouting at the television when the Dodgers lose. If that's what adults call truly living, you might as well shoot me right now.

Yeah, I know, I'm exaggerating again. I suppose that's something you're going to have to get used to if you're going to be my little sister or brother—and strange as it seems right now, I guess you are.

Fast Forward to the end of October. It had been more than a month since the day Janie and Bob first brought Kenya into the restaurant. Looking back, I can see now that Mom and Dad were getting more and more hung up on the idea of adoption. Suddenly, we were seeing Janie and Bob every weekend, and Mom seemed to spend the entire time with Kenya in her arms. There was a book about adoption on Dad's bedside table, and a big envelope came in the mail for Mom from some adoption organization.

But at the time, I barely noticed any of that stuff. I was too busy doing schoolwork and hanging out with Marc, Lauren, Forest, and Noah. Marc was pushing the Student Council to start a Social Service Committee that would get the school involved in community service. All my spare time was spent attending Student Council meetings, circulating petitions, and contacting local agencies about possible projects.

Then Saturday morning rolled around. I was sitting on my bed, writing letters for Amnesty International and listening to the radio, when Mom knocked on my door and walked in.

"Could you at least wait until I say 'Come in'?" I asked.

"The door was ajar. I could see you weren't busy."

"Yeah, right," I said, not looking up. "I'm only writing a letter to the president of Colombia, asking him to remove a man from death row. Do you have any air mail stamps?"

Mom sat down beside me and very gently brushed

my hair out of my eyes. I stopped writing and looked at her. She hadn't touched my hair in a long time, not since I told her I want it on my cheek and lay off, okay? But this was different, a sort of "are you in there?" kind of touch.

"What?" I asked.

She fingered the edge of my mussed bedspread. "Janie called. Their birthmother knows a girl who's almost six months pregnant and wants to put the baby up for adoption."

I didn't say anything. I mean, what was I supposed to say?

"We were thinking we might meet with her," Mom continued. "How would you feel about that?"

I stared at her. "I guess you figure I'm a lost cause so you might as well start over with a new one, huh?"

Mom looked startled. I was startled, too. I hadn't planned to say that. The words just popped out. I wasn't sure if I believed them or not.

"It's not like that," Mom said.

I looked down at my letter. "Then how is it?"

"Remember when Janie told us that she found herself staring at babies, wanting to hold them?" Mom asked. "I know how she feels because I've felt that way, too."

"You?" Mom seemed much too busy with the restaurant and the house and her PTA meetings to be swooning over babies.

She took a breath. "We never meant for you to be an only child, Sara. We tried to have another baby a year after you were born—in fact, at one point I thought I was pregnant. Turned out it was a tumor. I had to have a hysterectomy."

"You had a hysterectomy? You never told me that."

Mom shrugged. "I didn't see the point. Besides, I wanted you to feel good about being an only child. I still want that."

"Only I'm not going to be an only child," I said, jumping up to turn off the music. "Not if you adopt a baby."

"Hold on, Sara," Mom said. "We're just discussing it, that's all. Besides, I thought you'd be thrilled. You're always telling us we don't do enough to help solve the world's problems. Well, according to Janie, this girl just broke up with an abusive boyfriend. She has very little money, no support system. The couple who adopt her baby will be helping the child and her."

I thought it over. I knew I should be happy. After all, I was totally in favor of adoption. And finding out that my parents weren't as selfish and closed-minded as I'd thought was a pleasant surprise.

But something was bothering me. I know you're probably thinking it was jealousy, Future Sibling, but that wasn't it. If anything, I'm eager to share their attention. I mean, Mom and Dad are in my face constantly. Anything that keeps them off my back is a definite plus.

But a baby? My parents are forty-two years old, and unlike Janie and Bob, they act like it. I can't imagine them getting up for late night feedings, carrying a kid around in a backpack, and chasing him around the playground. And what about when the child gets older? Mom and Dad practically had a stroke when I told them I wanted to pierce my navel. How are they going to handle the stuff Kid Number 2 throws at them? I mean, we're talking the 21st century. The latest fashion statement will probably be surgically attaching a third arm to the middle of your chest or something.

But I think deep down what really bothered me was the part about my mother's hysterectomy. Why hadn't she ever told me that she and Dad had wanted more than one child? It made me feel left out, angry. I wondered what else they were hiding from me.

"I want to ask you something," I said suddenly, turning from the boom box. "Was I an accident? I mean, did you plan to have me?"

"Yes, of course we did, Sara. Why would you think otherwise?"

"I don't know. Your life sounds like it was so perfect before I was born—living on the beach, Dad playing in a band. Why would you want to change that?"

"It wasn't as perfect as you think," Mom answered. "We were ready for a change. After all, we were twenty-eight years old. It was time to grow up."

Is that what growing up means? I wondered. Having babies and settling down to a life of middle-class mediocrity? In that case, I think I'll have my tubes tied.

"You were very much wanted, Sara," she said again. "I want you to know that."

I felt better, a least a little. I gazed at Mom, sitting there in a blue flowered dress, her graying brown hair tucked behind her ear, and tried to picture her with a newborn. It wasn't easy.

"Then why do you want another child?" I asked.

She didn't answer directly. She just looked at me and said, "You're growing up so fast. If we adopted a baby, you'd be fifteen years older than him—more like a parent than a sister."

I couldn't believe what I was hearing. Mom and Dad

are always haranguing me about how I'm still a child and I don't have all the answers, and reminding me that until I'm eighteen, I have to do what they tell me. Now, for once, Mom was talking about me like I was a responsible adult.

I thought it over. Maybe adopting a baby wasn't such a bad idea, I decided. Mom, Dad, and I could raise the child together. We'd all take turns changing diapers, getting up for late night feedings, walking the baby in the park. Little by little, Mom and Dad would stop seeing me as their teenage kid and begin viewing me as an equal partner, an individual.

I was starting to get excited, Mystery Baby, imagining all the positive ways I could influence your life. I pictured myself taking you to rock concerts, film festivals, political rallies—all the stuff Mom and Dad would never go to in a million years. I dreamed of cooking vegetarian food for you, buying you cool clothes, and teaching you rap songs. Maybe I'd even start a band and become the star Dad never was. Then you'd be that little kid dancing in the grass at the outdoor concert, and I'd be the one up on the stage mesmerizing the crowd.

"It might be fun to have a little sister or brother," I said at last.

Mom stood up and hugged me. It was something we hadn't done for a while and we were both a little out of practice. We stumbled apart and stood looking at each other.

"So I'll call Janie and tell her we want to meet Iris, all right?" Mom asked.

"Iris," I repeated. It was an old-fashioned name, but

a pretty one. I wondered if she looked like the flower she was named for—tall, slender, graceful.

Suddenly, I felt a little nervous. It was one thing to imagine an infant sort of magically appearing in our lives, and quite another actually to sit down with a living, breathing pregnant person and ask her if we can have her baby.

"What's she like?" I asked. "How old is she?"

"Her name is Iris Boone, that's all I know," Mom said. "I guess we'll find out the rest soon enough." She laughed nervously, and I knew she was feeling apprehensive, too.

Then Mom turned, and I saw that Dad was standing in the hallway, watching us through the open door. I wondered how long he'd been there. Mom nodded at him and he smiled. Then she walked out of the room, leaving me with this weird, scary, exhilarating, nauseating feeling that my life was about to change in some massive, mind-boggling way. But whether it would be for better or for worse, I had absolutely no idea.

October 30

Hey Babe,

Welcome to the present—well, sort of. You see, even though the stuff in my last three entries is all part of the story of your life, I didn't actually sit down and write about it until today. That's because I only just met your birthmother, Iris. And because it was only yesterday over tacos and Mexican sodas at Cafe Lobo that Janie urged us to keep a journal of the adoption for you to read someday.

Brroing! That was the sound of my head spinning. I'm still having trouble dealing with the fact that we're going to adopt a baby, Iris's baby. You.

I was jogging through the kitchen, grabbing a Pop Tart as I stuffed my geometry homework in my note-book, when Mom gave me the news. She had called Janie, who had called Megan, who had called Iris. We were meeting her in Palm Tree Park in downtown Laguna Verde at four o'clock.

"Wow," I said.

"Exactly," Dad agreed. He was leaning against the counter, still in his robe, drinking coffee.

"So what do we talk about?" I asked.

"Janie gave me some idea of what to ask," Mom said. "Mostly we just want to get to know each other, find out Iris's circumstances, and figure out if she's really serious about placing the baby."

"Some girls accept money from more than one couple, then turn around and keep the child," Dad explained. "Sometimes they aren't even pregnant. We want to make sure this girl isn't trying to take us for a ride."

Can you believe that? My father is so suspicious. Here I am feeling sorry for this girl who's six months pregnant, broke, and alone, and all he can think about is protecting himself.

"Do you want us to pick you up at school?" Mom asked.

Somehow I had a feeling that riding over to the park with Mom and Dad would just stress me out. "I'll take the bus," I said, shoving most of the Pop Tart in my mouth.

Mom and Dad looked at me. I turned to face them. Mom took both our hands. "Do you think we're doing the right thing?" she asked.

"We haven't said yes to anything yet," Dad replied in his usual infuriatingly literal way. "This is an introductory meeting. We can back out at any time." He squeezed her hand and dropped it.

But Mom was still holding mine. Fortunately, my mouth was too full of Pop Tart to answer her question. I say fortunately because I didn't know the answer. I didn't have a clue. With a shrug, I pointed to the clock, grabbed my books, and hurried out the door.

On the way to school I stopped at the library and checked out a book about childbirth. It's filled with photographs of the entire nine months, from the moment the sperm wiggles its way into the egg to the instant the baby pops out between its mother's legs (something that still doesn't seem possible, even after seeing numerous color photos).

Outside the library, I spotted Lauren riding by on her bike. She looked great, as usual, her perfect Japanese-Italian skin all brown and smooth against her white and purple bicycle shorts and windbreaker. I ran after her, waving my book. She saw me and pulled over.

"Check this out," I said, opening the book to a photo of a woman in labor, grunting and straining. "Doesn't this look like fun?"

Lauren wrinkled her nose. "If I ever drop a kid, I want massive drugs." She grabbed the book out of my hand and turned it over. "What are you doing with this? Are you writing a report or something?"

I shook my head. "Remember I told you about those friends of my family who adopted a baby? Well, my parents are thinking about doing the same thing."

"Are you serious?" Lauren asked. "Why?"

I told her about my mom's tumor and hysterectomy.

"Wow, that's intense. So now they're talking about adopting?"

"It's gone beyond that," I said. "We're meeting with a birthmother this afternoon. She's six months pregnant."

"You're kidding! Who is she? I mean, how did they find her?"

We walked along, Lauren pushing her bike beside me, while I told her everything I knew, which wasn't much.

"How do you feel about all this?" she asked.

"Okay, I think. How would you feel?"

"Pissed off. I've already got two sisters I have to share my stuff with. Besides, I remember when Monique was born. Mom used Trish and me as live-in baby-sitters. It sucked."

"Oh," I muttered, wondering if that's the way it would be at my house.

We crossed the street and walked across the school lawn. "You'd better hide that book," Lauren said suddenly.

"Why?"

"You don't want any nasty rumors to get started, do you?"

I gazed at her blankly. "What do you mean?"

"Like that you're the one who's pregnant." She looked at me. "You're not, are you?"

"Don't be ridiculous," I said, shoving the book into the bottom of my backpack. "Besides, I would have told you if anything like that had happened."

"Well, I should hope so. If you and Marc so much as touch lips again, I expect a full report."

"Yeah, yeah," I said, dismissing the possibility with a wave of my hand. Marc and I hadn't even been alone together since that night at his house. I think the whole thing had freaked him out as much as it had me. I mean, up until then, we'd considered each other good friends, nothing more. Anyway, doing the wild thing was the last thing on my mind these days. I had other stuff to think about—like how I felt about becoming an instant big sister.

All of a sudden, Lauren burst out laughing. "I just thought of something," she said. "If your parents adopt this kid, people on the street will see you with it and just assume it's yours. And then they'll think your parents are the grandparents!"

"Oh God," I groaned. "I'll die."

"And wait till you find out what a pain in the butt it is to have a toddler around," Lauren said. She began a long story about the time Monique was playing beauty shop and put Lauren's pet mouse in the dryer, but I wasn't listening. I was beginning to wish I'd never talked to Lauren. Just minutes ago I'd been leafing through the childbirth book, feeling awed by the mystery of life and excited about the possibility of being entrusted with the upbringing of a brand-new human being. Now I felt as if my life was about to end. Not a great feeling, especially since I was only eight hours away from meeting your birthmother and you.

I got to Palm Tree Park early, about quarter to four. Mom and Dad hadn't arrived yet, so I wandered through the park, watching the little kids riding their tricycles and swinging on the jungle gym. I saw a girl not much older than me holding a small boy up to the water fountain. In the past, I would have assumed she was his babysitter. Now I wondered if she might be his mother, or possibly even his big sister?

Then it occurred to me that Iris might already be in the park, and if I was lucky I could get a look at her before we actually met. I'm not sure why that appealed to me. Partly, I was just curious to see what she looked like, of course. But there was more. I think I suspected that by catching her unaware I could learn something important about her—her true feelings about the baby inside her, maybe, and whether or not she was going to be straight with us.

God, I thought, I'm starting to sound like Dad. I decided that if I did find Iris, I wouldn't spy on her. Instead, I'd walk right up and introduce myself, put her at ease, and prepare her for meeting Mom and Dad.

I walked through the park, checking out everyone I passed. But aside from the toddlers, their caretakers, and the homeless people sleeping under the trees, the place was almost empty. Then I spotted a pregnant woman walking down the path. It had to be Iris. She was much older than I'd expected—in her mid-thirties at least—with dark hair pulled back and a long, horsey face.

I headed toward her, ready to introduce myself, but at the last second I chickened out. There was something about her expression—aloof, smug—that unnerved me. Instead, I walked past her, then turned and fell into step behind her.

What is my problem? I wondered. I doubled my speed and moved closer. Talk to her, I told myself. Just talk to her.

Suddenly, she spun around and faced me. "Why are you following me?" she demanded.

I froze. I could feel my face getting hot. "I—I—" I stammered.

"Oh, all right, *here*," she muttered. She pulled a quarter out of her purse and thrust it into my hand. "And don't use it to buy drugs."

"No," I squeaked, drawing back. "No, you don't—"

"Sara, over here!"

I gasped and turned. Mom and Dad were standing on the grass, waving. I dropped the quarter and practically sprinted over to them.

"We told Iris to meet us at the bench by the fountain," Mom said. "Are you ready?"

"Who was that?" Dad asked, motioning toward the woman, who had stooped down to pick up her quarter.

"No one," I mumbled, grabbing his arm. "Let's go."

We walked together to the fountain. And then I saw her, sitting up very straight at the end of the bench with her hands in her lap. She looked older than me, but not quite an adult. She was tall and big-boned, large but not fat. In fact, I couldn't even tell she was pregnant. She had a wide, pretty face with green eyes, milky skin, and straight reddish-brown hair. She was wearing jeans, a black leather jacket, and a loose-fitting yoked blouse made with patches of mismatched material.

"Iris?" my mother asked.

She stood up and smiled a small, closed-mouth smile. "Yeah." Her voice was deep and throaty. "Hi."

"I'm Marty Dewherst," Dad said in his cheerful restaurant voice. "This is my wife, Jeanette, and our daughter, Sara."

"Hi," I said. "This is a pretty bizarre way to meet, huh?"

Dad shot me a look, but Iris laughed. "Hell yes!" She stopped, realizing what she'd said. "I'm sorry. I mean, yeah. Yeah, it is."

Mom and Dad laughed uncomfortably. "This bench is so small," Mom said brightly. "Maybe we should sit at a picnic table."

We moved eagerly to the nearest table. I think we were just grateful to have something to do. Mom and Dad sat on one side, Iris on the other. I hesitated, then sat beside her.

"So . . . tell us a little about yourself," Dad said.

Iris stared down at her hands. "There's not much to tell. I grew up in the desert, outside Indio. My family's still there, but I left around a year ago."

"Do your parents know about your pregnancy?" Mom asked.

"No," she said flatly, "and they won't either. I'm eighteen. I can do what I like."

I wondered what was up between Iris and her parents. She was only three years older than me, but she was on her own. I was dying to ask her, but I knew Mom and Dad would disapprove.

"Where do you live now, Iris?" Dad asked.

"In Ellwood. I've got an apartment above the dry cleaners where I work."

Ellwood is a small city on the other side of the mountains. It's only about twenty miles from Laguna Verde, but it's like another world. L.V. is rolling hills, ocean views, and red tile roofs; Ellwood is hot dust, pickup trucks, and fast food restaurants. The tourists flock to Laguna Verde, but Ellwood is where the people who work in the tourist hotels actually live.

"And the baby's father?" Mom asked gently.

Iris played with the beaded leather bracelet on her wrist. "We broke up," she said. "At first I thought I could raise the baby alone. But then I realized I was just being selfish. I wanted someone to love me, someone I could love back. I figured a baby would take care of that." She put a hand on her stomach and looked up. "This kid needs a lot more than I can give. He needs a mother and a father, a house, a yard to play in, a future. He *deserves* it."

I looked at Iris. Her cheeks were flushed and her eyes were shining. For the first time since we'd shown up, she looked totally alive.

"Maybe we should tell you a little bit about us," Mom suggested. Then she and Dad launched into a long story about their life together, with a big emphasis on how hard they've worked and all the material possessions they've accumulated—stuff like a successful restaurant, a house three blocks from the beach, and a daughter with a 3.85 grade point average. Like *I* was one of their possessions.

I was just about to break in and set Iris straight about our family when I noticed her eyes were closed and her face had turned kind of ashy. I stared at her, wondering if I should say something. Then suddenly, she slumped forward against the table.

"Iris!" I gasped.

Mom stood up and grabbed her shoulder. "Iris, are you all right?"

She opened her eyes and sat up fast. "Yeah. Yeah, I'm fine," she said, brushing her hair out of her eyes. "I'm just . . . I—I think I forgot to eat lunch."

"Good heavens, you're eating for two," Dad scolded. "You can't skip meals."

"I don't usually. I had to come up with the rent today, but I get paid tomorrow. I'll be okay."

"Tomorrow is a long time from now," Mom said. "You need food now." She looked around. "There's a coffee shop across the street. I'll get you a sandwich."

"I'll come with you," Dad said, jumping up. "Sara,

you stay with Iris, okay?" I knew he wanted to be alone with Mom so they could talk about Iris, but I didn't care. I wanted to stay behind.

I waited until they were out of earshot, then I threw my leg over the bench and turned to Iris. "You sure you're okay?"

She nodded. "I get dizzy sometimes, but it passes."

"Hey, don't mind that big rah-rah speech my parents gave about how great they are," I said. "Sometimes they forget there's more to life than making money."

Iris smiled. "Yeah, but there's no life at all without it. Anyway, you have to think about things like that when you're raising a family. It's like I told Eddie, the kid comes first."

"Eddie was your boyfriend?" She nodded. "Didn't he want it—the baby, I mean?" I asked.

Iris twisted the beads on her bracelet. "He was mad as hell when he found out I was pregnant, but he stuck around. I'll give him that. He wasn't going to let it change his life though. He was out partying every night and he wanted me there with him. It just wasn't going to work, you know?"

I didn't really, but I nodded. I couldn't imagine what it was like to be living on your own, without any parents to tell you what to do. It sounded like heaven. "I wish I could do what you did—just leave home and get my own place—but my parents would never let me. How'd you convince your mother and father to let you do it?"

"I didn't ask them," she said. "I just left. They probably haven't even noticed I'm gone."

"You mean you haven't talked to them since?" I asked.

She smiled her closed-mouth smile. "I've got six brothers and sisters, my father's a drunk, my mother works nights. They were probably happy to have one less mouth to feed."

Okay, Mystery Baby, so maybe right now you're feeling kind of bad, thinking you come from a pretty screwed-up family. But let me tell you, your birthmother is one amazing person. I mean, I've never known anyone like her before. Unlike me, she's experienced the world outside of perfect, plastic Laguna Verde, and it's made her tough, brave, and totally independent.

I wanted to tell her that, but I didn't know how. Instead, I pointed at her bracelet and said, "Where'd you get that? I love it."

"You do?" She looked pleased. "I made it."

"No kidding?" Now I was really impressed with Iris. "Have you ever tried to sell your stuff? This is much nicer than most of the jewelry they have at the weekend craft show at the beach."

She shrugged. "Maybe someday. Right now I just make clothes and jewelry for myself."

Well, it turns out she made the blouse she was wearing, too, and believe me, Mystery Babe, I was blown away. I mean, I could never do that kind of thing. I don't have the talent, not to mention the patience it takes to imagine an object, plan the design, and then create it. I barely have the patience to sew on a button.

I was still oohing and aahing over Iris's blouse when Mom and Dad returned with the food. They'd bought a ham and cheese sandwich for Iris, and potato chips and sodas for everyone. Iris unwrapped the sandwich and took a big bite. She was trying to play it cool, but I could tell she was really hungry.

Dad waited until Iris had finished half the sandwich. Then he said, "We have a question about your boy-friend—your *ex*-boyfriend. In California, the birthfather has to sign a document either consenting to the adoption or agreeing to relinquish his rights. If he doesn't, the adoption might not go through." He paused. "Do you think he'll sign?"

"When we broke up, Eddie told me the baby's future was up to me," Iris said. She nodded. "He'll sign."

Mom and Dad looked at each other. Then Mom took a breath and said in a shaky, excited voice, "Iris, if you'll let us, we'd like to adopt your baby."

Gee, folks, thanks so much for talking it over with me first. I mean, I was pissed. What if I had hated Iris? But of course I didn't, so it seemed pointless to say anything—at least not right then and there.

We all looked at Iris, waiting to hear her reaction. She was staring at her hands, twisting her bracelet. Then she looked up and said, "I'd like that. And I'd like Sara to be the baby's big sister."

Maybe Mom and Dad weren't thinking about me, but Iris was. I caught her eye and grinned. She smiled back.

Then Dad raised his can of Diet Coke. "To the baby," he said.

Mom, Iris, and I lifted our cans of soda. "To the baby!" I exclaimed. I clinked my can against Iris's. Soda sloshed out of the hole and splashed across the table, drenching her potato chips. Iris and I burst out laughing.

Mom looked startled; Dad looked annoyed. But when they saw Iris and me falling all over each other gig-gling, they chilled out and joined in.

Two elderly women standing beside the fountain turned and looked at us. They probably assume we're a family, I thought—and then I realized we *are* a family, only not in the way those women imagined it. We're all bound together because we care about you, Mystery Baby, and about your future. And the weird thing is, even though we don't even know you yet, all four of us already love you.

November 4

DEAR MYSTERY BABY,

Things are happening fast—too fast. Mom and Dad have spent the last week cleaning out the spare room and filling it with baby equipment. Not just regular everyday Kmart stuff either; we're talking a teak crib, a fabric-covered rocking chair that adjusts to two positions, and a teddy bear that plays prerecorded womb noises.

I keep thinking back to that night Janie and Bob were over and Mom and Dad said how I spent the first few months of my life sleeping on a mattress on the floor because they were too broke to buy a crib. I'll bet I didn't have a jogging stroller, a black and white mobile guaranteed to appeal to a newborn's developing eyes, or the entire line of Fisher-Price toys. So how come you—the second kid, the kid who isn't even my parents' flesh and blood—rate all that, huh?

Okay, Mystery Baby, I apologize. That crack about flesh and blood was out of line. A baby doesn't have to come out of a woman's body to be her child. Still, it doesn't seem right that a mother would love an unborn adopted baby more than her living, breathing biological daughter, does it?

I'm probably crazy to think something like that, but then how else do you explain what's going on around here? Like what happened today when Marc asked me to go to the Pro-Choice Coalition benefit concert down in L.A. later this month.

I was excited for a lot of reasons. For starters, I want to show my support for a woman's right to choose in any way I can, and since there's no way Mom and Dad would ever let me volunteer at a family planning clinic, this is the next best thing. Second of all, the concert is going to showcase lots of cutting-edge L.A. bands, and I'm completely stoked to see it.

And last—but definitely not least—Marc asked me to go, and I happen to know he didn't ask Lauren, Forest, or Noah. Which means he doesn't view this as a group event but as an actual, bona fide date. Which means maybe that close encounter we had last summer wasn't simply the result of raging hormones, but actually had some sincere emotion behind it. Which means, wow, I guess I'd better figure out how I feel about him, and what better way to do that than by spending an entire day together in L.A.?

So I asked my parents if I could go.

"No," my father said before the words were even out of my mouth.

"What?" I cried. "Why not?"

"Because you're too young to take the train down to L.A. without an adult. And because I don't want you spending the day at an unsupervised rock concert, especially not one being sponsored by a bunch of pro-choice groups."

"Oh, I suppose you'd like it better if it was sponsored by the religious right," I said.

"I wouldn't let you go to their rock concert either," Dad replied with an infuriating smile.

Then Mom got in the act. "Sara, believe me, you don't want to get mixed up in that kind of controversy. It's a red-hot issue, and whenever either group stages a protest, the opposition shows up to make a scene."

"This isn't a protest," I pointed out. "It's a fund-raiser. An outdoor rock concert."

"It's going to attract oddballs," she said. "I don't want you in a position where you might get hurt. That's the bottom line."

That's when I lost it. "You never let me do anything I want!" I shouted. "You hate me!"

"How can you say that, Sara?" my mother exclaimed. "We love you."

"Oh, yeah?" I cried. "Then why is it you're spending all your time and money on some unborn kid, but when I ask for just one little thing, you won't give it to me?"

I didn't get to hear their lame excuses, because I ran out of the house and rode my bike to the mini-mart. Then I called Lauren and asked her to meet me at the playground.

The playground is actually Escondido Park, a mostly forgotten city park at the end of a dead-end street. There's a cracked tennis court without a net, a rusty jungle gym, and a creek lined with sycamore and euca-lyptus trees. According to my dad, the city plans to fix up the park next year, which means it will soon be crawling with toddlers, joggers, and church groups. But for now it's mostly used by high school kids who want to make out, get stoned, or just hang out and talk.

I found Lauren sitting cross-legged on the grass inside the jungle gym. I crawled in beside her and told her what was going on.

"I wouldn't even bother to ask my parents if I could go to the concert," Lauren said. "I know they'd never let me."

"Maybe I'll go anyway," I said. "I'll just tell them I'm going to the library and then I'll take off."

"Go for it." She handed me a stick of gum, then lay back on the grass with her legs hooked over the bottom rung of the jungle gym.

I lay beside her, blowing bubbles and watching the clouds drift by. "I'm starting to have these weird thoughts," I admitted, glancing over at her. "Like what if the baby turns out to be really stupid? Iris seems pretty intelligent, but who knows for sure? And what about Eddie? He sounds like a real jerk."

"That doesn't mean he's stupid," Lauren pointed out.

"Maybe not, but Janie said he's abusive to Iris, so he's gotta be pretty sick. What if his kid turns out the same way?"

Lauren snorted a laugh. "Come on, Sara. You think the baby's going to pop out of Iris and start punching people?"

God, what was I saying? I hate people who label other people stupid or bad or losers just because they've made mistakes in their lives. Like my parents who, believe it or not, support the death penalty. But the truth is, most criminals had horrible childhoods that messed them up for life. They're screwed up, not genetically programmed to be bad.

Still, I couldn't stop thinking about you, Little Fetus, and worrying that you had something wrong with you. "What if the kid is ugly?" I said. "I mean a real dog?"

"That would be tough, especially if she's a girl," Lauren agreed. "Society can deal with an ugly guy, but watch out if you're female. Of course, there's always plastic surgery."

"But what if the baby's deformed or something?"

'Then you don't have to adopt him, do you?" Lauren asked.

I frowned. "You mean, if he had something wrong with him we could just give him back to Iris?" I shook my head. "No way. That would be too cruel. I mean, she doesn't have enough money to raise a healthy kid. How would she handle one with problems?"

"But if the kid comes out with some major handicap," Lauren said, "you're going to get stuck dealing with it for the rest of your lives."

I could feel my stomach twisting into a knot. Who knew what we were getting into? This adoption could be a total disaster. And yet at the same time, deep down inside, I was almost hoping something would be wrong with the baby. Then Mom and Dad would be sorry they'd screwed up our perfect little family. They'd look at me and think how good they'd had it when I was an only child. And then I'd know they loved me best.

I felt ashamed to be thinking thoughts like that, and I had this crazy feeling that if Lauren looked me in the eye right then she'd see what a crappy, selfish person I was. So I jumped up and started climbing the jungle gym. Lauren climbed after me.

"Do you know Cody Zeller?" she asked.

"I've heard his name. He's in our class, right?"

She nodded. "He's adopted."

I perched on the top bar and gazed across the tops of the sycamore trees. "How do you know that?"

"In Sociology we were talking about nature versus nurture. You know, like what's more important in shaping a person's character—their genes or their environment? And then we had to write a paper about it, and I guess Cody wrote about being adopted. So Ms. Geiger asked him to do an oral report on it, and he did."

"What did he say?" I asked.

"All kinds of stuff. He got in touch with his birth-mother this past summer. You should talk to him."

Wow, I was getting excited. I've never known anyone who was adopted—except Kenya, of course, and he's not exactly ready to have a thought-provoking conversation. So maybe I *will* talk to this Cody guy. Only I can't just walk up to him and say, "Lauren tells me you're adopted. What's it like?" He'd probably just blow me off. And even if he didn't, the whole conversation would end up feeling formal and rushed and just plain awkward.

Hmm. Somehow I've got to figure out how to get friendly with Cody Zeller in a way that will make him just naturally want to open up with me. But how? I don't know yet, Kiddo, but I'm working on it.

When I got home from the playground the house was quiet, so I figured Mom and Dad were out. Good,

I thought. I don't want to deal with them now. But as I started down the hall, I heard them in the spare room. I froze, then tiptoed to the door and peeked in. Mom and Dad were up on stepladders, paint brushes in hand, stenciling a border of teddy bears across the wall.

I pulled back and leaned against the hallway wall. Mom was in the middle of a sentence. I closed my eyes and listened.

"—the way she used to climb out of her crib and appear in the living room, all smiles, saying to us, 'I thought you might be lonely.' "

Dad laughed. "She was quite the little manipulator."

Mom's voice: "She still is."

Dad: "Yes, only now it's not so cute. That storming out of the house trick isn't going to work. She's not going to that concert, period."

Mom: "She's going through a stage, Marty. Anyway, she's probably confused about the adoption. After fifteen years, she's suddenly getting a sibling. That's a lot to adjust to."

Dad: "But I thought she was all for it."

Mom: "I think she is. But doubts and worries are natural—we have them all the time, right? Besides, you know Sara. She thrives on melodrama."

Dad: "She thrives on trouble. Sometimes I think she sits up at night planning new ways to make our lives difficult."

Laughter. Then Mom said, "She's growing up fast. Just two more years and she'll be off to college."

"It's so strange the way things work out," Dad said. "I thought when Sara left home, we'd be alone. Instead, we're starting all over again as new parents."

Mom: "Isn't it wonderful?" I could hear the smile in her voice.

Next I heard footsteps, shuffling feet on plastic, a sigh. I peeked around the door. Mom and Dad had climbed down from their ladders and were hugging each other. I stood there watching them, feeling shut out, alone. Then tears filled my eyes and a sob caught in my throat. I turned and hurried to my room.

Mom knocked on my door a few minutes later. I had stopped crying and was lying on my bed listening to my Walkman. Naturally, she wanted to know where I'd been.

"Around," I said, pulling, the earphones off. "Now I'm back. Who cares?"

"We do," she told me. She sat on the edge of the bed. "Sara, we're not going to give you permission to go to that concert. But that doesn't mean we don't love you—or that we love Iris's baby better."

Was she telling the truth? The way Mom and Dad had been talking, it sounded as if they could hardly wait to get me out of the house so they could start over with a new kid.

"Did you notice how I said 'Iris's baby'?" Mom asked. She smiled and shook her head. "I don't even think of the child as ours yet. It's too soon. It just doesn't seem real."

"Those toys you bought look pretty real," I said. "And all those clothes and the furniture and the stroller."

Mom didn't answer. She just looked at me. Then she said, "Sara, if we adopt this baby, it has to be something we do together as a family."

"Yeah? So?"

"It's normal to have doubts," Mom said, "to be confused and uncertain. But if you truly don't want this adoption to happen, I want you to tell me right now. Because if we don't have your support, we're not going through with it. We'll simply call Iris and tell her we've changed our mind."

I tried to imagine my parents returning all those toys and baby clothes to the store, turning the nursery back into a guest room, giving up their dream of having a second shot at parenting. "If I say no, you'll blame me forever," I told her. "I don't want that kind of guilt."

My mother looked exasperated. "If we go through with this adoption without your support, *you'll* blame *us* forever. Now please, Sara, just tell me how you feel—do you want to adopt Iris's baby or don't you?"

I felt a surge of power. All I had to do was open my mouth, and the whole thing would stop right there. With one little word, the lives of four people—and one person-to-be—would be changed forever.

But I couldn't do it, Mystery Baby. Why? I'm not really sure. Maybe it's because I've been looking at those photographs in the birth book I checked out of the library and you do seem real to me. Maybe it's because I've been writing you these letters. Or maybe it's because I know your birthmother now and I like her. I keep remembering the way she smiled when I got excited about her bracelet, the empty look in her eyes when she told me that her father's a drunk, and how we laughed together when I spilled the soda. I can't just dump her now, and I can't dump you.

"Yes," I said softly. "I want to adopt Iris's baby."

Mom smiled. "I knew it. That's what I told your father."

If you know everything I'm thinking and feeling, Mom, why did you even bother to ask me? That's what I was thinking, but I didn't say it. Let Mom and Dad think what they want. They'll never understand me.

Mom stood up. "We're setting up an appointment for Iris with an obstetrician," she said. "We'll be going with her. Do you want to come along, too?"

See? That's just an example of how little my mother knows me. How could she imagine I wouldn't want to come? I mean, this is my chance to see Iris again— and to learn a little more about you, Mystery Baby. "I'm coming," I said.

She left the room and I put my headphones back on and turned the music up loud. I think I was hoping I could blast all the confused thoughts out of my head. It didn't work then and it isn't working now. I think I'll go to bed. Are you sleeping now, too?

Sweet dreams, Little Sib. Good night.

November 9

DEAR BABYCAKES,

I saw you today! True, the image was black and white, scratchy and shadowy, and half the time I couldn't tell your butt from your head. But it was you. And guess what? You're a girl! Well, that is, we couldn't see a penis, which means you're either a girl or you had your leg in a funny position. Anyway, the important thing is, you're normal and healthy. And real, very real.

As you can guess by that first paragraph, we went with Iris to the obstetrician this afternoon. Mom and Dad picked me up from school and we drove to a medical office building near Laguna Verde Hospital. The doctor's name is Robert Horloff and I asked Mom if he was the obstetrician who delivered me. But no, it turns out they picked Horloff for one reason and one reason only—because he agreed to accept the health insurance the state provides for low-income people like Iris. A lot of doctor's won't even treat poor people because the state doesn't pay very much, so naturally I figured

Horloff must be a good guy—you know, committed to empowering low-income women and all. Boy, was I wrong.

But wait, I'm getting ahead of myself. Let me start at the beginning. We were standing there outside the building, waiting for Iris, when all of a sudden this huge Harley chopper came roaring into the parking lot. On the front was a tall, muscular guy with a mustache, and on the back was . . . Iris. The guy pulled the bike into a space, turned it off, and took off his helmet. Then he climbed off and helped Iris off. As soon as she pulled off her helmet, he grabbed her and gave her a big, wet French kiss.

Wow. I mean, they looked so hot, like characters in a movie. He had long, brown hair pulled back into a ponytail, a handsome face with deep-set eyes, and arms that were completely covered with tattoos. He looked exciting and dangerous, and I knew my parents would have a stroke if I even talked to someone like that.

When the kiss ended, Iris pointed toward us. The guy turned, squinted, and grunted something. Then he sauntered out of the parking lot and headed down the street. Iris walked over to join us.

"Who was that?" my father asked. He was trying to keep his voice light and cheerful, but I could tell he was tweaked.

"That's Eddie," she said, "the baby's birthfather."

Mom frowned. "I thought you two broke up."

"We did, but he came to my apartment last night and we had a long talk." Her eyes were shining and her skin glowed. She smiled. "Don't worry. He's in favor of the adoption one hundred percent."

Dad didn't look convinced. "Is he going to be involved? If he is, I think we need to meet him and talk things over."

"Maybe he'd like to come to see the doctor with us," Mom suggested, but Iris explained that Eddie had to meet someone downtown. He's a motorcycle mechanic, she said, and he came into the city to give a friend an estimate on a repair.

So we went inside. Dr. Horloff's waiting room was small and shabby. The cloth plants were dusty, and the magazines were out-of-date. The receptionist gave Iris a stack of medical forms to fill out, and she gave Mom and Dad a stack of financial ones (they're paying for any expenses the state doesn't cover). We all sat down and they set to work.

"Can you believe this?" Iris asked, turning to me. I looked at the form. It listed about a hundred medical problems, everything from shortness of breath to lung cancer. You were supposed to check any that applied to you. "I've never heard of half this stuff," she told me.

"If you don't know what it is, you probably haven't had it," I replied.

She laughed and drew a line through all the blocks marked No. Then she crossed out one and checked yes. "This isn't exactly a disease," she said. I looked at the question. *Do you have any tattoos?* it said.

"You have a tattoo?" I asked. "Where?"

"On my chest. It's a flaming heart with Eddie's name inside it. He's got one with my name in it."

God, it must be incredible to be on your own. My parents would never in a million, trillion years give me permission to get a tattoo. "Did it hurt?" I asked.

"Hell, yes. I had to toss back about ten shots of tequila to get me through it."

Iris leaves me awestruck. She's done things I've never even dreamed of. She's really lived.

She went back to filling out the forms, and eventually the nurse called her name and we all trooped into an exam room. Iris sat on the exam table. There were no other places to sit so Mom, Dad, and I stood against the wall, feeling awkward but trying to look as if hey, we go to pregnant women's obstetrician exams all the time.

First the nurse made Iris go behind a curtain and change into one of those horrible paper robes. Then she took blood from Iris's arm and finger, and led her down the hall for a urine test. When they came back, Dr. Horloff appeared. He was a middle-aged man with bad posture, black, thinning hair, and the kind of dark, five-o'clock shadow that never completely disappears, even after a shave.

He ignored Iris and walked directly to my father to introduce himself. They shook hands, and then my father introduced Mom and me. Finally, he turned to Iris. "Good morning, young lady," he said. "Is this your first prenatal visit?"

Iris nodded.

Horloff shook his head disapprovingly. "You have to start taking responsibility for your situation. There's a child growing inside you and he can't take care of himself. Now, do you know the date of your last period?"

"Uh, no," she said. "I—I didn't plan to be pregnant and so . . . I guess I just tried to ignore it."

"Ignoring it won't make it go away," Horloff said, as

if we didn't all know that. "Now lie down on the table and we'll see what we can do to determine a due date."

Iris lay back, and the nurse instructed her to put her feet in the awful metal stirrup things. She did, and there was an instant, just before Horloff draped a paper sheet over her, when I caught a glimpse of her swollen stomach. Reality check! With her clothes on, Iris hadn't look pregnant, but now I could see that she most definitely was. And I kept thinking, there's a fetus inside there. An almost real, live baby.

Iris gazed at the ceiling as Horloff took a tape measure and reached beneath the paper sheet to measure her stomach. "Pretty much what I suspected," he said, glancing over at us. "She's approximately twenty-eight weeks along. So . . ." He squinted at the calendar on the wall. "That means we'll estimate the due date as January 23."

The combination of Iris's rounded belly and the due date made it all seem so much more real than it had before. January 23, I kept repeating in my head. I'm going to meet my new brother or sister on January 23. That's you, Mystery Babe.

Horloff's voice brought me back to the present. "Have you ever had a PAP smear, Iris?" he asked.

She shook her head.

"Well, it's about time you did." He pulled a plastic contraption out of a drawer and turned to us. "Could you just step outside for a moment?"

We filed into the hall and Mom said, "I suppose it won't be long until you're going for your first PAP smear."

"Oh, come on, Jeanette, she's only fifteen," Dad said, as if I wasn't even there.

"I read an article that said girls should get checked out when they're sixteen or become sexually active," Mom told him.

"Well, she's certainly not sexually active!" Dad exclaimed.

Ha! I bet Dad's head would spin if he knew how close Marc and I had come to doing it. And if we go to the Pro-Choice concert down in L.A., who knows? I might need that PAP smear sooner than Dad realizes.

Mom and Dad were still talking about me when Horloff called us back inside. Iris glanced at us, then back at the ceiling. She looked kind of out of it. Then Horloff smeared blue glop on her stomach and picked up a little black box. He reached under her gown, and suddenly the room was filled with a series of static bursts, almost like gunshots. Mom and Dad looked at each other and grinned. Iris looked alarmed.

"What's that?" I asked.

"The baby's heartbeat," Horloff told me. "And it sounds just fine." He glanced at Iris. "Now sit up and we'll listen to yours."

She did as she was told and the doctor stuck a stethoscope to her chest. He listened a moment, then reached for her arm and lifted it up. There were some blue blotches above her elbow. "How did you get these bruises?" he asked.

Iris stared at her knees. "I don't know," she muttered.

"Tell me about the baby's father," he said, releasing her arm. "Are you having a relationship?"

"Yeah, sure. We were living together, then he moved out. But we made up. He's all for the adoption, don't worry."

"I'm not worried," Horloff said in a smooth voice. "Are you?"

Iris was starting to look annoyed. I felt like cheering. "What are you talking about?" she demanded.

"Have you taken any drugs during your pregnancy?" Horloff asked.

"No."

"Any alcohol?"

"No."

"Has your boyfriend been rough with you?"

"No. No way."

Horloff smiled a fake smile and told her the nurse was going to sign her up for a childbirth preparation class, plus give her a pamphlet on diet during pregnancy. "Now, Iris, the nurse will take you for your ultrasound." He turned to us. "I'd like to have a word with the three of you before you join her."

Iris left with the nurse, and Horloff turned to us. He gave us a big speech about how he wasn't one hundred percent convinced that Iris isn't using drugs or alcohol. He said she didn't show any signs of being a hard drug user, but he wouldn't rule out marijuana use. According to him, the baby feels and sounds healthy so everything is probably fine, but he said if we could question her a bit more—discreetly, of course—that would be good.

"The ultrasound will give us more information on the baby's health," he said. "And I drew blood so we can test her for syphilis and other sexually transmitted diseases." He smiled. "All in all, she seems like a healthy girl. I don't think you have anything to worry about."

Mom and Dad looked pleased, but I felt like puking.

All three of them were talking about Iris as if she were a horse we were thinking of buying. I felt like asking Horloff if he'd checked her teeth.

Then he led us into a darkened room, but he didn't come in with us, thank God. I looked around. Iris was lying on another exam table. Next to the table was some sort of machine, and beside that was a TV monitor and a computer keyboard.

I walked over to Iris. I tried to imagine how I'd feel if I were in her position. Alone, probably intimidated, maybe downright scared. So I leaned over and whispered, "Horloff is an ass."

She laughed. "I felt like a piece of meat on a butcher's table."

"Have you ever had a PAP smear, young lady?" I said, mimicking his pompous voice.

She snickered. "He's got cold hands and bad breath."

Out of the corner of my eye, I noticed Mom and Dad standing by the door, watching us. I knew they were wondering what we were laughing about. Forget it, folks, I thought. You wouldn't understand.

We were still giggling when a young woman in a white lab coat walked through the door. She tapped some keys on the keyboard, smeared some more blue glop on Iris's stomach, and picked up a sort of wand. As she touched it to Iris's belly, a grainy black and white image appeared on the TV monitor.

"Can you see it?" the woman asked, pointing to the monitor. "That's the baby's head . . . there's a leg . . . there's the other leg . . ."

I stared at the screen. Slowly, my eyes started to adjust. The grainy blobs turned into a small, curled-up human form. You, Mystery Baby. It was you!

"Let's see . . ." the woman said thoughtfully, moving the wand to change angles. "I can't get a good view of the genitals. I don't see a penis, which might mean it's a girl, but I can't really—oh, look, it's moving!"

We stood and stared at the screen, mesmerized, as you raised your hand and put your tiny thumb between your lips.

"He's sucking his thumb!" my father exclaimed.

"Yes," the woman said, "the touch of the thumb against the lips precipitates a slight sucking reflex."

"Oh, she's so precious!" my mother squealed.

"That's my baby," Iris said in a hoarse whisper.

I had been so overwhelmed by the moving image of you, Baby, that I had almost forgotten about Iris. Now I looked at her. She was staring at the monitor with her mouth slightly open. Her eyes were shiny and moist. She looked positively blown away. And I was reminded that this was *her* doctor's appointment, and *her* ultrasound, and most of all *her* baby, and we were just visitors, three guests that she had brought along for the ride.

I stepped back, suddenly a little embarrassed. But Mom and Dad didn't look embarrassed at all. If anything, they seemed kind of worried. They exchanged a troubled glance, and my father reached down and squeezed Mom's hand.

And then I realized what was going on. They didn't like hearing Iris call the image on the monitor "my baby" because that meant she was getting emotionally attached to it. And if she gets too attached, she just might decide to keep it.

God, how typically self-centered of my parents to think something like that. It almost made me wish Iris *would* decide to keep you, Little One, just to prove to Mom and Dad that despite what they think, money does not always equal power.

But then I realized something else. If Iris kept you, Mystery Baby, I'd never get a chance to see you in the flesh, never get to hold you, or make you laugh, or take you up in the oak tree in my backyard and show you the sun rising over the sea.

Listen, Kiddo, I want your birthmother to do what feels right to her. I really do. But deep down, I can't help hoping she'll want to let us raise you. Because I can't think of anything I'd like better than to be your big sister.

November 10

After the ultrasound, the woman in the white coat printed out some pictures of you, Baby. She gave two to Iris and two to us. I talked Mom and Dad into giving me one, and it's sitting on my bedside table now. It's not the one of you sucking your thumb—they wouldn't part with that one—but I love it anyway. I can see your profile (I imagine you're looking thoughtful and curious), your chest, and your arm, which is stretched out toward the world that awaits you. I wish I could reach out and take your hand, but I guess I'll have to wait a few months for that.

The lab tech told us you look healthy and normal, so I suppose I can stop worrying that you're going to have three eyes or nine fingers. And Mom and Dad and Dr. Horloff can lay off Iris about the drinking and the drug use—although it turns out she wasn't one hundred percent straight with us when she told Horloff she was clean. But hold on, I'm getting ahead of myself, as usual.

After the appointment was over, we went to the pharmacy on the first floor of the medical building so Mom and Dad could buy Iris her prenatal vitamins. Then Dad gave her a lecture about riding a motorcycle while she was pregnant. She pointed out that she didn't have a car and if she hadn't gotten a lift into Laguna Verde on Eddie's cycle, she would have had to take the bus (which takes two hours to travel twenty miles and has a much lousier suspension system than Eddie's Harley). So Dad said maybe they could help her buy a used car and they'd discuss it at their first appointment with the adoption lawyer, which they hope to schedule sometime next week.

Then we walked outside and everybody just stood there trying to think of something to say. Iris looked kind of lost and sad—no surprise after being poked and prodded and cross-examined by Horloff the Horrible—and I was wishing we could spend a little time with her, maybe reassure her that we loved her baby as much as she did and we were going to give him (her?) a really good home. But all Dad said was, "Will your boyfriend be back soon?"

"Yeah, sure," she told us.

"Maybe we should wait and meet him," Mom suggested.

"No," Iris said, and I could tell by the look in her eyes that she couldn't think of anything she'd like less. "I mean, I'm not exactly sure when he'll be back. And then we have to drive across town so he can pick up some parts." She shrugged. "You'd better go."

So Mom and Dad headed for our car, promising to call Iris in a couple of days. But I wasn't ready to leave yet. I wanted to tell her that maybe Mom and Dad didn't know how she was feeling right now, but I did. I mean, watching her lying on that exam table, it was easy to put myself in her place—pregnant, scared, confused, and with some smug, condescending stranger's hand between my legs. I don't know if I could have handled it as well as Iris had. I probably would have ended up shouting at Horloff to get his filthy hands off me, and then dissolved into tears.

But there was another reason I didn't want to leave Iris yet. I wanted to get to know her better, to learn more about her life, and maybe get another look at Eddie and her together. I wanted to understand what it felt like to be independent, with an apartment, and a job, and money of your own. Imagine being able to eat and sleep when you want, party every weekend, have sex whenever the mood hit you. That was Iris's life, and being near her was like being in the same room with people who are smoking dope. It gave me a contact high.

I followed Mom and Dad to the car and said, "I have to draw some graphs for my Economics paper and I need to buy a pack of felt-tip pens. Can you drop me off at Staples? I'll take the bus home."

After the usual lecture ("Don't talk to strangers, don't walk on the backstreets, be back by dinnertime"), they agreed. They let me off at the corner of State and Las Posas. As soon as they drove away, I jogged back to the medical building, hoping Iris and Eddie hadn't left yet. My heart soared when I spotted Iris sitting on the curb beside the Harley, alone.

"Hey, girlfriend," I called, strolling toward her, "what's up?"

She squinted up at me. "What are you doing here?"

Iris didn't look pleased to see me, and suddenly I felt kind of stupid. What was I doing there, anyway? "I don't know," I mumbled. "I guess I just wanted to make sure you're okay."

"Why wouldn't I be?" she asked.

Oh, Lord. I was beginning to wish I'd gone home. "No reason," I said. "It's just . . . Horloff and my parents were treating you like you're some stupid hillbilly."

Iris kicked a pebble with her motorcycle boot. "Probably cuz that's what I am."

"Are you serious? You're independent, strong, brave—" I looked at her. Her eyes were red. "Have you been crying?" I asked.

"No," she said, looking away.

I ran my hand across the cycle's handlebars, trying to think of something else to say.

"Eddie will be back any minute," she said, glancing at me. "He doesn't like anyone touching his cycle."

"Oh." I could tell when I wasn't wanted. I turned and started to walk away. Then something stopped me. Maybe I could tell Iris wasn't serious about wanting me to leave. Or maybe I just hoped she wasn't. "Listen, you wanna get something to eat? It won't take long. My treat."

Iris stood up and looked up and down the street. Eddie was nowhere in sight. She leaned down and carefully adjusted the strap on her motorcycle boots. "All right," she said at last. "But I have to be back in twenty minutes."

I smiled. "Okay. Good."

"Why did you call me brave?" she asked suddenly. "I'm scared stiff."

That shocked me. "Scared?" I asked. "Of what?"

"Of everything. Giving up the baby. Not giving him up. I don't know. I thought everything was settled. Then Eddie showed up last night . . ." She motioned toward the medical building. "And then in there, when I saw the baby . . ." Her voice trailed off and she shook her head.

"Look, you have to do what feels right to you," I said. "But even if we raise your baby, that doesn't mean you'll never see him again, does it? I mean, you can come over to our house anytime you want." I didn't know if that was true, but it sounded reasonable. After all, why shouldn't a birthmother stay in touch with her adopted baby, even help raise him if everybody agreed? Anyway, I was certain we could work something out.

Iris stood up and smiled at me. "Where do you want to eat?"

I figured there was a cafeteria in the hospital, but Iris said hospitals give her the creeps. So I suggested The Spot. It's a greasy spoon popular with kids from the high school and junior college. It's got waitresses with hair nets, jukeboxes on the tables, faded photos of Laguna Verde on the walls—sort of like one of those fifties theme restaurants, only The Spot is the real thing. It's downtown, about a five-minute walk from Horloff's office.

"Okay, let's go," Iris said, straddling the Harley.

"We're taking the bike?" I asked, amazed and hopeful.

"Sure, why not? Hop on."

I climbed on behind Iris. She put on Eddie's helmet and handed me hers. It was too big, but I wasn't about to complain. The cycle started with a roar, and before

I could have second thoughts, we were driving out of the parking lot. I slipped my arms around Iris's waist and held on tight.

Wow, Mystery Baby! It was my first time on a motorcycle, and I loved it. The wind was blowing in my face, the smell of the engine filled my nose. Even when we were going twenty, it felt like fifty. It was awesome! And the fact that I knew my parents would have heart failure if they could see me made it even better.

I shouted directions into Iris's ear and soon we were pulling into the parking lot behind The Spot. Iris hooked the helmets to the bike and we walked inside. It was the usual afternoon scene—a couple of cops and construction workers drinking coffee at the counter, and the rest of the tables filled with students. The jukebox was blasting some goofy country song, and a few kids were laughingly singing along.

We claimed a booth that was being vacated by some kids from the junior college, and sat down. I saw a couple of girls I know from my English class. They stared curiously at Iris, probably wondering who this mysterious stranger was. I knew she looked different than my other high school friends—older, a little tougher, very cool. It felt good to be with her.

Then the waitress came over and we ordered— grilled cheese for me and a burger and fries for Iris.

"There's not much I can eat here," I told her. "I'm a vegetarian."

She looked amazed. "Really? Don't you like meat?"

"I used to, but now I don't even think about it."

"I don't think I could live without burgers," she said. "And ribs with barbecue sauce. Umm!"

"If you saw the inside of a slaughterhouse, you might

64

change your mind." I told her a little about the video Marc had brought back from one of his PETA meetings. I could tell by the look in Iris's eyes that it was getting to her. I imagined how great it would be if I could convince her to become a vegetarian, and how impressed Marc would be.

Iris flipped the song racks on the jukebox. "I know what you mean about killing animals," she said with a grimace. "It used to make me sick when my father went hunting and came home with a deer strapped to the front of the car."

Just then, the food came. Iris stared at the hamburger. "I'm sorry, but ever since I got pregnant, I've been craving burgers," she said. "Do you mind?"

I shook my head and Iris attacked the burger like a puppy pouncing on a bone. I guess it's going to take more than one afternoon to turn her into a vegetarian, but that's okay. I want to spend more time with her.

"You know, it's weird," I said. "A few days ago, I was feeling really jealous of you. But now I feel . . . I don't know, like we're in this together or something."

Iris looked skeptical. "Jealous of me? Why?"

"Because you're giving my parents something they really want. There's nothing I can give them—except myself, and they definitely don't want that."

Iris snorted through her nose. "What I have to give is no big deal. Believe me, anyone can get knocked up."

I had to laugh. Unlike my proper, uptight parents, Iris gets right to the point. "You're right," I said, sipping my soda, "anyone can get knocked up. But then you have to deal with it. That's why I said you're brave. I mean, I probably would have had an abortion and gotten on with my life. But what you're doing is a lot harder, and a lot more generous."

Iris poured ketchup on her fries. "The only reason I didn't think about getting rid of the baby is because I didn't think about the baby, period. I just sort of pretended it didn't exist. That is, until I started showing and Eddie noticed it. Then I had to face facts, only by that time it was too late to do anything except get on with it." She smiled, a little sadly I thought. "Do you still think I'm brave?"

"Yes, I do," I told her. "You could keep the baby, but you're giving her to us just because you want her to have a better life. That's got to be hard. Plus, you have to put up with my parents and with Horloff the Horrible. For that, you deserve a medal."

I thought my Horloff the Horrible crack would make her laugh, but Iris stared down at her hands and twisted her bracelet. "I know I haven't always done what's best for the baby," she whispered.

"Oh, come on, don't let them intimidate you!" I cried. "You haven't got anything to apologize for."

"Yes, I have. The truth is, I did drink during the first couple months. Eddie expected me to go out partying with him every weekend, and that meant getting bombed. But I felt so sick to my stomach, I couldn't keep up with him. Then finally I just stopped altogether."

"What about drugs?" I asked.

"I smoked some grass, that's all," she said. "Then I stopped that, too. I'll bet you don't think I'm so wonderful now, do you?"

But I do. I mean, I'm not happy Iris drank and smoked dope while she was pregnant, but I understand it. And I bet it really took a lot of willpower to stop, especially if Eddie was pushing her to get wasted with him. Which is what I told Iris. And what really killed me was that she looked relieved and almost grateful, as if she truly cared what I thought.

We ate the rest of our food in silence, and then suddenly Iris put down her burger and stared at the clock on the wall. "It's almost four-thirty? If Eddie gets back and I'm not there—" She slurped down the rest of her soda and stood up. "Let's go, okay?"

"All right, all right, relax," I replied, pulling my wallet out of my backpack.

The instant I put the money on the table, Iris was out the door. It was as if she was scared of what Eddie might do if she was late, and I wondered what really went on between them. Did he hit her? I just couldn't believe it. Iris was too strong and smart to put up with crap like that.

I wanted to talk to her about it, but I wasn't sure how to start, and before I could figure it out, Iris was on the Harley and revving the engine. I jumped on and we roared into the street.

While we drove, I closed my eyes and tried to imagine what Iris's weekends had been like before she got pregnant. I pictured Eddie and her at some roadside bar, tossing back tequila and dancing to the driving beat of the house band. Then I imagined them getting on the Harley and roaring through the mountains, whooping and hollering and stoned out of their minds, until finally they headed for home where they made wild, passionate love on the living room floor.

Then I thought about my pathetic little life—school, homework, bed, school, homework, bed, and maybe a movie, a trip to the beach, or a tame high school party on the weekends. Talk about a dead-end life. I mean, I know that alcohol, drugs, and unprotected sex can be deadly, and it's not like I want to end up in rehab or anything, but just once I wish I could throw caution to the wind and do something wild, something dangerous, something that my parents have never done and would never do in a million, trillion years.

But before I could figure out what that might be, we were squealing into the medical-building parking lot. Eddie was nowhere in sight.

Iris killed the engine and climbed off. She was relaxed now, and smiling. "I had a good time," she said. "Thanks for asking me."

"No problem. I just figured after what you went through, you needed a break."

Iris nodded and reached in her pocket. "I made you something. I was going to give it to you earlier, but I didn't get a chance." She pulled out a bracelet like the one she was wearing and handed it to me.

I was blown away. I mean, it's so cool that Iris made me one just because I told her how much I like hers. Plus, it pleases me to imagine her in her apartment, stringing beads and thinking about me.

And then suddenly, I had an inspiration. I asked Iris if she and Eddie wanted to go to the pro-choice concert down in L.A. with Marc and me. She hesitated, but then she said she would ask Eddie. I was so excited at the thought of going with them, I didn't even remember that I wanted to stick around until Eddie showed up. I just took off jogging across the parking lot, shouting, "Call me!" over my shoulder.

Oh, Mystery Baby, I am so stoked! If Iris and Eddie

decide to go to the concert, my parents are sure to let me go, too, if only because it will mean I can spend some time with Eddie and report back to them on everything I learn. And how cool will it be to spend the day with Iris and Eddie? Who knows? Maybe we'll get inspired and do something really crazy, like go to the Griffith Observatory and reenact the final shoot-out from that old James Dean movie *Rebel Without a Cause*. Now that's what I call wild and dangerous!

November 17

Dear Babes,

I met Cody and I think I like him. He's awfully Sierra Club for my taste—you know, the kind of guy whose idea of fun is hiking to the top of a mountain in the pouring rain just so he can say he saw some kind of endangered species of lizard in the wild that he could have seen any day of the week at the zoo—but that's okay. The important thing is he seems pretty together, which is good because Mom and Dad have started subscribing to a magazine for families who are involved in adoption, and reading it has started me thinking a lot about the problems adopted kids have to face.

Like it turns out there are plenty of people who are prejudiced against adopted kids, partly because the media loves to do stories about the tiny minority of adoptees who grow up to become rapists and mass murderers, all the while ignoring the vast majority who turn out totally normal. And of course there's the mistaken belief (which, as you know, I've been guilty of) that adopted kids will inherit all sorts of bad traits from their birthparents—like if their birthfather is in jail, then some people assume the kid is going to wind up being a criminal, too.

But aside from all the bogus stereotypes and prejudice, there are plenty of other problems adopted kids have to deal with. Like feeling they're second-best because their parents adopted them after discovering that they couldn't have biological kids. And suspecting they must be bad people, because otherwise why would their birthmothers have given them away?

Oh, Mystery Baby, I don't want you to have to deal with that stuff, but I guess you will. I just hope I can help you get past it, just like I hope to help you get past all the work-hard-don't-make-waves propaganda my parents are going to stuff down your throat. And then there's the way they're going to treat you like an insignificant child, even when you're almost an adult, just like they do with me. Like for example, this morning when they announced they were meeting with Iris and the adoption lawyer at nine o'clock.

"Nine o'clock?" I repeated. "But I'll be in school."

Mom was cooking scrambled eggs. She gave me some story about how Iris had off from work today and they needed to be back at the restaurant for the lunch crowd. "Plus, the lawyer had an opening this morning," she said. "It just seemed to make sense."

"Why didn't anyone talk to me?" I demanded. "We could have found another time."

"Honey, please, be reasonable," Mom said. "All we're going to do is meet the lawyer and go over a few legal details. It's not worth missing school for."

She tried to hand me a plate of eggs, but I ignored her and took a gulp of orange juice out of the carton.

She hates that. But I didn't wait around to hear her lecture. I just grabbed my books and left the house.

On the way to school, I thought about skipping second period and showing up at the lawyer's office. Boy, would Mom and Dad be surprised. But then I realized I had no idea what lawyer they're using or where his office is. So I was screwed. Thanks, folks.

As I walked across the school lawn, I saw Marc sitting on the front steps. He's not the kind of boy most girls would describe as their dream date—he looks kind of like a young Dustin Hoffman, only with shoulder-length hair—but he's got a real presence about him. I guess it's because he's so committed to changing the world, so directed, so knowledgeable. And unlike me, he doesn't let his emotions get out of control. He's calm, collected, and very, very sure of himself.

Marc stood up and waved when he saw me. "We did it!" he called.

I asked him what he was talking about.

"The student council met yesterday after school and voted to form a Social Service Committee. I'm the new chairman."

"Marc, that's great!" I gave him a hug and he squeezed me hard, which made my heart start to flutter.

"Of course, they won't let us do anything too political, not right away, anyhow," he said, "so we'll have to stick to charity projects for a while. Maybe sponsor one of those Save The Children things, something warm and fuzzy like that."

"That would be great," I said. "There are so many children out there who need help."

"Sure," he replied, stretching out on the steps, "but the really important thing about this committee is that it gives us legitimacy. The administration can't dismiss us as tofu-eating kooks anymore, and that means we can use our new clout to get some important stuff done." He reached into his backpack and pulled out a stack of papers. "Like this."

I sat down, and he handed me a sheet. It was a petition, demanding that the cafeteria offer healthy vegetarian alternatives to their typical meat dishes. "Marc, this is excellent," I said.

"A hundred signatures combined with a few more lunchtime protest demonstrations ought to make our beloved principal sit up and take notice," he said with a smile.

Marc kills me. He really knows how to make things happen. I suppose that's partly the way he's been raised. His parents were real revolutionaries in the sixties, and they still travel around the state participating in rallies and demonstrations for radical causes. They don't mess around, either. Marc once told me that between the two of them, they've been arrested a total of twenty-four times.

"About the pro-choice concert next month," I said.

He turned to me. "Yeah?"

"My pain-in-the-butt parents said I can't go, but I think I've figured out a way to change their minds."

"Don't tell them," he suggested.

I smiled. "I thought of that, but I've got a better idea. I invited Iris and her boyfriend to go with us. She's eighteen, and I think he's even older. My parents are dying to get some information about—"

"Who's Iris?" he broke in.

That surprised me, and it hurt a little, too. I'd told Marc all about my family's adoption plans. How could he have forgotten? But when I started to explain, he cut me off.

"I just forgot her name," he said. Then he laughed. "You sure she wants to go to a pro-choice concert? I mean, she's a walking advertisement for the Right-to-Lifers."

A pregnant teenager at a pro-choice concert. I hadn't thought about it until now. Still, why not? "Just because Iris decided to go ahead with her pregnancy doesn't mean she doesn't support a woman's right to choose," I told him. Not that I actually knew Iris's opinions on the subject, but I just couldn't believe she was anti-abortion.

Marc put his elbows on his knees and frowned. "I just thought we were going to be alone," he said. He glanced at me. "I've got my learner's permit, you know. I'm supposed to have a licensed driver in the car with me, but I figure I can get away with it just this once . . ."

I pictured Marc and me driving down to L.A. together, just the two of us. I felt weak all over and I kept forgetting to breathe. Suddenly, I wished I had never asked Iris and Eddie, which was kind of a crappy thing to think, I know, but what can I say? Marc makes my brain freeze. "Iris and Eddie are licensed drivers," I said lamely.

"Okay, okay," Marc said, getting to his feet. "So we'll take them if it means so much to you." He touched my arm. "Don't forget the petition," he said. Then he walked away.

Terrific. If Iris and Eddie go to the concert, Marc

will be pissed, and if they don't, I'll have to lie to my parents plus risk getting stopped by the cops because Marc doesn't have a real license. It's all too much to deal with, so I've decided to put it out of my mind and concentrate on the petition.

Which is how I finally found a way to talk to Cody. It was lunchtime, and I was walking around the lawn outside the cafeteria, looking for people who might be sympathetic to my cause. A lot of kids eat out there when the weather is nice, which it was. I saw Jake Halsey and his jock friends sitting at a picnic table, throwing Jell-O squares into the air and trying to catch them in their mouths. At one point, Jake collected about fifteen squares in his mouth, which he then spit out at his girlfriend. Charming.

I decided to write off Jake and the jocks as hopeless cases and walk on. Then I spotted Cody Zeller, sitting alone under a tree. He was munching on a sandwich and gazing up through the branches.

"Have you thought of seeing a chiropractor about that crick in your neck?" I asked.

Okay, so maybe it wasn't a great line, but I figured it might make him chuckle. Instead, his head whipped around and he stared up at me, startled. I could tell from the look in his eyes that he was a million miles away.

"I'm sorry," I said, feeling foolish. "I didn't mean to bother you."

He smiled then, a broad, friendly smile, and I took a second to look him over. He's a tall, bearlike guy with wide shoulders and muscular legs. He's got thick, curly blond hair, clear blue eyes, and the kind of tan most people around this town have in the summer, not the winter. He was dressed in jeans, hiking boots, and a plaid flannel shirt over a black T-shirt; and he wore a small, turquoise stud in his left earlobe.

Cody took the same second to look me over. I wondered what he saw. A skinny girl with short, brown hair and a too-wide mouth? A political activist in a faded Question Authority sweatshirt? A goddess straight out of his dreams? Yeah, sure.

Then he said, "You're Sara, right? I didn't recognize you without your pig nose."

I laughed. "It was a new look I was trying out, but it really wasn't me. I'm thinking of going for something a little more green." I knelt down and pulled up a handful of grass, then held it in front of my face. "What do you think?"

"Very attractive. But did you know there's a spider crawling toward your ear?"

I let out a shriek and began batting wildly at my face. Cody stood up and calmly flicked something off my cheek. "Got it," he said.

I stopped batting and stood there, feeling stupid. 'Thanks," I mumbled. Then I asked him what he'd been looking at in the tree when I walked up.

"A cedar waxwing," he said.

"A what?"

"It's a bird." He looked up. "It's still there. See it?"

I followed his pointing finger and found myself gazing at a kind of bird I'd never seen before. It was brown with a tall tuft on its head, yellow on its tail, and dark brown markings around its eyes that made it look like it was wearing a mask. "It's beautiful," I said.

He nodded. "See the red spots on its wings? They

look kind of like wax, which is why it's called a waxwing."

"Are you into bird watching?" I asked.

"Not really. I just like animals in general."

"Then maybe you'd like to sign my petition." I handed it to him.

He read it carefully. "I'm not a vegetarian, but I'll sign. A little more variety in that cafeteria couldn't hurt." He scribbled his name on the first line and handed it back to me.

"Thanks," I said. "But if you're into animals, why do you want to eat them?"

"Animals eat other animals," he said simply. "That's the natural order of things."

"Maybe in the wild that would be true," I said. "But we're thinking animals and we can make a choice. Why take the life of an innocent cow or pig or sheep when you can get along just fine eating fruits, grains, and vegetables?"

"Because I like cow with french fries and pig with eggs," he replied with a shrug.

"That's just it," I said, my voice rising. "Everybody has been so brainwashed into thinking they can't survive without meat that we've created a huge industry devoted to raising and slaughtering animals. But in the process, we're cutting down the rain forests and destroying land that could be used to grow crops—enough crops to wipe out all the hunger in the entire world."

Cody didn't answer. He just looked at me and smiled. I could feel my cheeks getting hot. "I get a little carried away sometimes," I muttered.

"I like that in a thinking animal," he said. He sat

down and reached into his backpack. "You want a peanut butter cookie?"

So I sat down and took one. We spent the next twenty minutes arguing about the world's problems. According to Cody, eating meat isn't necessarily a bad thing. The problem is that we've turned meat production into a huge industry in which human beings are distanced from the animals they consume. He says if we really want to live in harmony with nature, we should be hunters and gatherers. Then he told me about these African tribes who hunt animals with spears and eat nuts and berries that they find in the bush. They do so well that they have lots of time left over to sing, dance, and tell stories. Plus, they barely make a dent in the ecosystem.

I don't know if I buy his argument—I mean, is killing a wild pig with a spear morally superior to killing one in a slaughterhouse—but it was certainly interesting to talk to him. Unlike the majority of people in this school, he actually seems to have a brain.

Anyway, the bell finally rang and we had to go to class. Then Cody said that since he signed my petition, I had to sign his. I asked him what he was collecting signatures for, and it turns out he's involved with this group that's trying to save Howorth Ranch.

"What's that?" I asked. "I mean, I've heard of it, but I don't know anything about it."

"It's a thousand acres of land up in the mountains that's been left to the city," he explained. "Only about a hundred acres of it was ever used as ranch land. The rest is pure wilderness."

"Sounds beautiful," I said.

"It is. Only now the mayor is talking about selling

part of it to a real estate developer." He stood up and slipped his backpack over his shoulder. "We're not going to let that happen."

If the determined look in Cody's eyes was any indication, the mayor might as well give up. I have a feeling Cody would try to stop the bulldozers with his bare hands if he had to. He might even succeed.

"Okay, where do I sign?" I asked.

"I don't have the petition with me," he said. "But I've got an idea. How about if we go for a hike on the ranch this Saturday? You can sign the petition then."

Mystery Baby, I've never been on a hike in my life. It's not that I don't like nature. I've just never been into dirt and sweat. But I do want to get a look at Howorth Ranch. Besides, I hadn't had a chance to talk to Cody about being adopted yet, and I figured a nice, long walk in the mountains would give me the opportunity. So I said yes.

Now I keep obsessing about Saturday and wondering what I should wear. Are overalls and Doc Martens appropriate outdoorwear? And what if I get bitten by a rattlesnake or eaten alive by a mountain lion? That would be an extremely unjust end for a committed vegetarian like me, don't you think?

Hmm. I think my mother might have a pair of hiking boots. I'm going to go look in her closet.

November 18

It's six o'clock and my parents are in the dining room eating dinner with Janie, Bob, and Kenya. I'm sitting in my room, trying to make sense of things. Of course my parents have been in here about fifteen times, asking, encouraging, then demanding and ordering me to come out and join them for dinner. Too bad, folks. You're like slave owners on some pre-Civil War plantation, thinking you can control the lives of everyone around you. Well, you may be able to boss your employees around, and Iris too, now that you've talked her into signing those papers, but you're not going to dictate to me.

Mystery Baby, you're probably wondering what's going on. Well, it's like this. Yesterday I arrived home from school, feeling as light and free as that cedar waxwing Cody and I had seen hopping around in the tree. Marc had called the first meeting of the Social Service Committee for that afternoon, and it looked like the committee was going to be a huge success. Of course, since no one else even knew about the meeting, only Marc, Lauren, Forest, Noah, and I showed up. Marc said he liked it that way because we all think alike, and he wouldn't mind one bit if no one else ever came to the meetings because then we could do whatever we wanted—but he was just kidding, of course. He's going to publicize the meetings in the school paper from now on.

Anyway, between the five of us, we had already gathered twenty-eight signatures for our petition. We decided to stage another protest demonstration at lunch next week to keep the subject fresh in the students' minds. Then Marc proposed that our next project should be to pressure the administration to add a multicultural World History course to the curriculum, and we all agreed. Finally, I reminded him about his idea to sponsor a child through one of those Save The Children organizations, and he put me in charge of doing the research.

So there I was, lying on the living room sofa with my feet up, writing in my journal and enjoying the fact that I was the only one home, when suddenly Mom and Dad walked through the door. I had forgotten that they'd hired a new hostess for the restaurant last week so they could have three nights a week off.

The first thing I did was sit up and slam my journal shut. It's impossible to think when they're around, let alone write. The next thing I did was ask them about the meeting with the lawyer.

"It went fine," Dad said. "We hammered out the basics of the adoption agreement, worked out the finances, signed a few documents."

I frowned. "Mom told me all you were going to do was meet the lawyer and go over a few legal details."

"That's what I thought," Mom said. "But the attorney said we should get things in writing now so there won't be any confusion later."

Can you believe it? I knew I should have gone to that meeting. "So what did you decide?" I asked.

"It's all pretty straightforward," Dad replied, sitting down in the leather chair and putting his feet on the ottoman. "We're going to give Iris a monthly stipend that will allow her to buy a used car and quit her job until the baby is born. During the next three months, we'll accompany her to her doctor's appointments and childbirth classes. And, of course, we'll be present at the birth."

I was happy about the monthly stipend. Now Iris will be able to concentrate on her jewelry-making and clothing designs. If she puts together some samples and takes them around to a few gift shops and the craft fair, she might make some sales. Then who knows? She might never have to go back to her job at the dry cleaners again.

I began making a mental list of all the places she could sell her stuff. I figured once she bought her new car, we could drive around to them together. Then I remembered the pro-choice concert. To tell you the truth, Mystery Baby, the thought of Marc maneuvering his way through L.A. traffic was making me a bit nervous. But if Iris drove us down in her car—hey, no problem. She's an outstanding driver; I'd seen that when we were on the motorcycle together.

"Mom, Dad," I began, "remember that pro-choice benefit concert down in L.A. Marc asked me to go to?

Well, Iris and Eddie want to go with us." That wasn't for certain yet, but I figured if I okayed everything with my parents first, Iris would be even more likely to say yes.

Dad put his feet down and sat up. "We said you weren't allowed to go to that concert," he told me. "I think we made that pretty clear."

"Yeah, but you said I was too young to take the train by myself. If we drive down in Iris's new car, I won't be on the train or by myself. I'll be with Iris and Eddie. Two adults."

Mom laughed a sort of you've-got-to-be-kidding laugh. "Iris and Eddie are hardly what I'd call adults. Not emotionally, anyway."

"Oh, I see. Well, if we're talking about emotional age, you two are in preschool," I snapped.

"Don't be smart, young lady," Dad said in a tense voice. "You're not going to that concert. You're not going anywhere with Iris, period."

I couldn't believe my ears. "What?" I gasped. "Why not?"

"Didn't you hear what I told you?" Dad said. "We're attending doctor's appointments and childbirth classes with Iris. That's it."

Mom nodded. "And after the adoption, we've agreed to keep in touch through letters only."

"What?" I cried. I thought back to that afternoon after Iris's appointment with Horloff the Horrible. I'd told her that just because she gave her baby to us to raise didn't mean she'd never see it again. In fact, I'd practically promised she could visit the kid whenever she wanted. "Did Iris agree to that letters-only rule?" I demanded.

"Yes, of course," Dad said. "The lawyer wrote down everything, and we both signed it."

"We're not making this rule to be unkind," Mom said, sitting beside me on the sofa. "We've read a lot of books, and talked to Janie and Bob and our attorney. Everyone agrees that after the birth, the baby needs to bond with us, and us with him. And Iris needs to get on with her life. That's why she's choosing adoption—because she's not ready to be a mother right now."

"But what about when the kid grows up?" I asked. "What if he wants to meet his birthmother? Or are you planning to tell him you found him in a Dumpster?"

"Don't be sarcastic," Dad shot back. "If the child wants to meet Iris someday, we'll be glad to arrange it. Until then, we feel it's best for everyone if we have only minimal contact."

"I just can't believe Iris went along with that," I said, shaking my head. "Not after what she told me outside Horloff's office."

Mom's head spun around. "What do you mean?" she asked. "What did she tell you?"

I hesitated. What had Iris said? All I could remember was something about her feeling scared. "That was a private conversation," I said at last. "If you want to know how Iris feels, ask her yourself."

Dad looked at me closely, as if he was trying to figure something out. "We were with you outside Dr. Horloff's office," he said at last. "There was no time to have a private conversation with Iris." He paused. "Have you been talking to her when we aren't around?"

I slouched into the corner of the sofa and hugged a pillow to my chest. "What if I have? So what? You do all kinds of things behind my back—like that first meeting with Iris at the park. You went off to get sandwiches and the next thing I knew you were telling her you wanted to adopt her baby. You didn't even bother to talk it over with me."

"We didn't have to," Mom answered. "When we came back to the park you two were chatting away like old friends. It was obvious that you liked her."

"Sara, listen," Dad said. "It's natural to feel sorry for Iris and want to help her. But becoming friends with her is not the way to do it."

I had to laugh. "Get a clue, Dad," I said. "I don't feel sorry for Iris. I envy her."

Mom looked stunned. "Iris has a boyfriend who abuses her, a dead-end job, and she's pregnant with a child she can't keep. What can you possibly find to envy about that?"

I didn't answer. What was the point? All Mom and Dad saw when they looked at Iris was a statistic—another unwed, pregnant teenager. They didn't see what I saw—a wild girl on a motorcycle, living life on her own terms, experiencing things her small-town parents couldn't even imagine. Okay, so maybe everything in Iris's life wasn't perfect. So what? At least she was out there living and learning, instead of spending her days trapped in a California tourist town, sheltered from reality by her overprotective parents.

Suddenly, I noticed my father was staring at me, studying me like a chess move. "In that private talk you had with Iris," he said slowly, "did she tell you anything about the first few months of her pregnancy? For example, did she mention anything about drinking or taking drugs?"

Can you believe it? What hypocrites! "I get it," I said, jumping to my feet. "You don't want me to get friendly with Iris—unless it benefits you." I threw the pillow down. "You don't give a damn about Iris, do you? To you, she's like a rental car that you drive until you get where you want to go, then you drop it off and forget about it."

My mother looked shocked, as if I'd slapped her. "That's unfair," she said. "We care about Iris very much, and we're doing our best to treat her fairly."

"Then why can't you do the same for me?" I shouted.

Dad looked astounded. "You don't think we treat you fairly? We give you everything—the roof over your head, the food you eat, the clothes you wear."

"Big deal. If I was on my own I'd be doing the things I want to do instead of hearing you order me around!" I ran to my room and slammed the door.

No one came after me, so I sat down at my desk and stared blankly at my Economics homework. Then I remembered that I had forgotten to use my most convincing argument for why Mom and Dad should let me go to the concert with Iris and Eddie—the one about how I could learn stuff about Eddie and report back to them. Only now I was glad I hadn't used it. I wasn't going to spy on Iris and Eddie for them. And I knew now I'd never betray Iris's secret about the drugs and alcohol she'd used during her first months of pregnancy.

I was still staring at my homework when Mom appeared at the door, carrying a bunch of books about adoption in her arms. She laid them on the corner of the desk and said, "I hope you'll look through these. They've been very helpful to us."

I nodded without looking up.

"Please try to understand, Sara," Mom continued. "We're glad you and Iris hit it off. I think part of the reason she decided to place her baby with us is because she knows you'll make a terrific big sister. But promise me you won't contact her behind our backs again. It's just going to make things more difficult for everyone."

The way Mom talked, all sympathy and understanding, you'd have thought her only concern was doing what was best for Iris and her baby. But I could read between the lines. This whole argument was about power and control. If Iris and I hung out together, we might actually start thinking. And as everybody knows, thinking leads to questioning, and questioning leads to—God forbid—rebellion. Then who knows what might happen?

Yeah, the more I think about it, the more I'm convinced that Mom and Dad want to keep Iris and me apart so we won't influence each other. I mean, to Mom and Dad, Iris is the ultimate bad girl. They probably think five minutes alone with her will turn me into one, too. And as for how I could influence Iris—who knows? They're probably worried I'll turn her into a radical feminist vegetarian who won't take any of their elitist crap.

Before Mom left, she asked me again to promise I wouldn't see Iris behind their backs. I nodded, but I had already made up my mind. I'm going to the prochoice concert—with Marc and Iris and Eddie, or with Marc, or even by myself if I have to. And Mom and

Dad won't have to trouble their tiny little minds about it, because they're never going to know.

Good news! Janie just came into my room to talk to me. She agrees with Mom and Dad that I shouldn't be hanging out with Iris, but she did admit that every adoption is different and she told me she'd heard of adopting families who became close friends with their baby's birthmother. There are even families who let the birthmother live with them before the birth and who stay in close contact with her afterwards.

Then Janie told me that the papers Iris and my parents signed in the lawyer's office the day before yesterday are informal agreements, not legal documents. The truth is, Iris can pretty much do what she wants until the baby is born and she signs the final consent papers. So if Iris wants to spend time with me, that's up to her, not my control-freak parents.

Deal with that, Mom and Dad, if you can.

November 19

Dear Em (little Embryo, that is),

I was up at eight this morning—a miracle for me—and downstairs fifteen minutes later. Mom and Dad were already up, scarfing down their usual Saturday morning breakfast of pancakes and—blech—bacon. I grabbed a bagel and headed for the door.

"Where are you going?" Dad called.

That's when I remembered I hadn't told Mom and Dad about my hike with Cody. But then why should I have to tell them every detail of my life? I'm fifteen years old, for God's sake, not five.

"Out," I mumbled through the bagel.

"Can you be a little more specific?" Mom said.

God, can you believe these people? They have zero interest in the mother of their child-to-be, but they're obsessively fascinated with the minute details of my day-to-day existence. "I suppose you think I'm sneaking off to meet Iris," I said.

"I don't know," Dad replied in his most infuriatingly calm voice. "Are you?"

"What is this—a prison camp?" I cried. They just kept staring at me, so I told them that this guy at school had asked me to go hiking and I'd said yes, so I was going, so butt out.

Well, the next thing I knew they were interrogating me like I was a suspected felon or something. Meanwhile, Cody and his mother drove up to the house and honked their horn. Instantly, Mom and Dad were out in the driveway, asking Mrs. Zeller all these painfully embarrassing questions like, "Are you sure it's safe for two teenagers to go hiking out there all alone?" and "Should I give Sara money for lunch?" Yeah, right, like there's a McDonald's in the middle of Howorth Ranch.

Anyway, they finally let me go, probably because they were planning to spend the day at a Baby Basics class and they wanted me out of the way. As Mrs. Zeller pulled out of the driveway, I turned to Cody. He was sitting across from me in the backseat, dressed like some kind of mountain man—a white SAVE THE RANCH T-shirt, khaki shorts with about twenty pockets, hiking boots, and a white baseball cap. I, on the other hand, was wearing a black ESPRESSO LOCO T-shirt, a pair of baggy men's boxer shorts with red hearts on them, and my ripped tennis sneakers (turns out my mom didn't own any hiking boots).

Cody smiled and I wondered if he was laughing inside. Suddenly, I was certain the only reason he'd asked me along was to watch me make a fool of myself. I could see the newspaper headline now: WIMPY LOCAL GIRL SLIDES OFF MOUNTAIN, PLUNGES TO HER DEATH. When the police questioned Cody, he'd just scoff, "What do you expect? She was wearing tennis shoes."

Fortunately, I didn't have a chance to continue my neurotic worrying because Mrs. Zeller kept up a steady barrage of perky questions as she drove—what do my parents do for a living, how long have we lived in Laguna Verde, how did Cody and I meet, and on and on until we were pulling off the freeway and turning down a winding country road. We drove past houses, barns, and grazing horses, until finally we took a left onto a narrow dirt lane full of ruts and mud puddles.

Centuries later—or so it seemed—the road ended and Mrs. Zeller stopped the car. We were in the middle of nowhere—just grass and trees and huge, gray boulders in every direction. There wasn't even a trail.

"Where are we?" I asked anxiously. I couldn't believe Mrs. Zeller was going to leave us there and drive away.

"On the north side of Howorth Ranch," Cody said. "Most of the ranch is surrounded by private property, which means no access. But I discovered this fire road. It leads into a section of the ranch that almost no one ever visits."

I tried to smile, but it felt like more of a grimace. Cody had said the ranch was pure wilderness, but I thought that at least meant a marked trail with maybe a portable toilet or two. Instead, we were stuck out here in the middle of total nothingness.

Cody got out of the car and slung a backpack over his shoulder. He didn't seem to notice that his hiking partner was having a panic attack. "Ready?" he asked cheerfully.

I climbed out and stood beside him. We watched as Mrs. Zeller backed up and turned around. "See you at noon," she called. Then she drove away, leaving a cloud of dust hanging in the air.

"You have to excuse my mother," Cody said, tramping off into the underbrush at top speed. "She's a family therapist and she's always trying to figure out what makes people tick. Her nonstop questions can get really irritating sometimes."

I stumbled after him, trying to keep up. We were heading uphill, moving through low-hanging oak trees, gray boulders, thick bushes, and grass. "It didn't bother me," I said. "I mean, I hate it when my parents cross-examine me, but this was different. I didn't get the feeling she was passing judgment on me or—ouch!" I jumped back and looked down at my shins. They were stinging and bleeding.

Cody stopped walking and came back to join me. "You stepped in a patch of thistle," he said, examining my legs. "When you hike, it's a good idea to wear long pants or thick socks like mine."

I wasn't wearing any socks at all. It just hadn't occurred to me. I leaned down to wipe away the blood when suddenly I heard a sound in the bushes, a loud CRUNCH, CRUNCH, like a wild animal was lumbering toward us. "What's that?" I whispered.

Cody grinned. "It's a big . . . scary . . . towhee!"

"A what?"

"A bird," he said with a chuckle. "It hops around in the underbrush, scratching for insects and seeds. It's noisy, but harmless."

A moment later, the bird appeared, small and brown. When it saw us, it let out a little peep and flew away. God, I felt like an idiot. I hoped Cody couldn't see how I was blushing.

I looked up to find out, but he had started hiking again. He was moving fast, never hesitating or stumbling, as if he knew exactly where he was going. I jogged after him, horrified of being left behind, tripping over vines and fallen branches and loose rocks as I went.

The air was crisp but the sun was bright, and pretty soon I was sweating. We were moving so fast, I couldn't imagine how Cody expected to spot any animals. Plus, there was no way I could make conversation. I was panting too hard.

I stepped over a large hole, forcing myself not to think about what might be living inside. Cody was getting farther and farther ahead of me. I scowled. At this rate, I was never going to find out his feelings about being adopted. I'd be lucky if I didn't loose sight of him altogether.

And then he finally paused. I figured he was stopping to talk to me, maybe apologize for walking so fast, but all he did was glance over his shoulder and call, "Sara, hurry up!"

That's when I lost it. I ran after him, gasping and sweating and shouting, "Who do you think you are—Indiana Jones? I thought we were going for a hike. But this—" I paused to gulp air. "This is more like a death march!"

Cody looked stunned. Then he grinned and said sheepishly. "I'm sorry. I guess I got kind of carried away. It's just that I wanted to show you this."

He pushed aside a tree branch and motioned for me to step forward. I did—and gasped. We were at the edge of a high ridge—it must have been a good five stories high—looking out over a vast canyon. Wispy white clouds lay below us, hovering above the canyon floor. An enormous hawk glided by, not fifty feet away from us. It gazed at us, unblinking, then plunged into the clouds and disappeared.

"I wanted you to see the canyon before the clouds burned off," he said. "They're usually gone by ten o'clock."

Suddenly, I wasn't mad anymore. Not a bit. "It looks like something out of a fairy tale," I breathed. "Like Camelot or something."

He laughed. "Nothing so romantic, I'm afraid. It's called Rattlesnake Canyon."

I wrinkled my nose, but he just laughed and said we should go down. I couldn't believe we could actually hike into the canyon and back in less than twenty-four hours, but he said he did it all the time. "Yeah, but I'm not you," I reminded him. Then I told him my fantasy about tumbling down a mountain and winding up on the evening news. He looked sympathetic, so I threw in the part about him scoffing at my tennis shoes.

"Come on, I'm not an ecological snob," he said. "I think Howorth Ranch should be open to everyone." He paused, and added, "Even city slickers in worn-out tennies."

Our eyes met and we smiled at each other. After that, things started to look up. We began walking down the ridge—slowly now—and we talked. I asked him how long he'd lived in Laguna Verde (five years), and that led into a question about where he was born (Indiana).

"How long did you live there?" I asked.

"About a week," he replied. "You see, my birthmother lived in Indiana and my parents went there to adopt me."

I loved the way he said it—not proudly exactly, but confidently, like he knew where he came from and where he was going. I had a sudden urge to tell him about you, Little Embryo, but then I decided against it. I didn't want Cody to think I was only hiking with him so I could pick his brain about adoption. I mean, that may have been true in the beginning, but it wasn't now. I was actually starting to like the guy. Besides, it was fascinating to hear adoption described from a different perspective—almost as if I was hearing it from you, Mystery Baby.

"You're adopted?" I asked innocently.

"I *was* adopted," he corrected. "Past tense. It's an event, not a condition."

I thought that over a second, then nodded. "You know, I used to think I must have been adopted," I told him. "I mean, it's like my parents and I come from different planets. We have almost nothing in common."

Cody paused to point out a pack of quail skittering through the underbrush. Then he said, "It's not like that. Not for me anyway. The stuff I inherited from my birthparents and the stuff I've picked up from my adoptive parents is all mixed up inside me."

"What do you mean?"

"Well, take for example last summer, when I went to visit my birthmother. At first, she seemed like a complete stranger. She's not into any of the stuff I am—hiking, surfing, kayaking. She doesn't even know how to swim. But after a while, I started to notice that her expressions are like mine, and so is her laugh. She likes quiet places, too, just like I do. Only for her it's her garden, not Rattlesnake Canyon."

That made sense to me. Like maybe we all start out with certain genetic traits and tendencies, but they get expanded and altered by our environment. "Have you stayed in touch with your birthmother your whole life?" I asked.

Cody explained that it was his parents who had stayed in touch. But a couple of years ago, he had become curious about his birthparents. At first, he was afraid to ask his mom and dad about them; he didn't want them to interpret his interest as a rejection of them. Eventually, he got up the courage to question them, and that's when he found out they had his birthmother's address.

"So I told them I wanted to contact her," he concluded.

"How did they handle it?" I asked.

"Okay at first. But when I wrote to my birthmom—Eileen is her name—and she wrote back, my parents kind of schized out." He shrugged. "You'd think being a therapist and all, my mom would have been able to deal with her feelings. But she was doing odd things—buying me big presents, wanting to take me on trips, like she was trying to impress me or something. My dad was just the opposite. He got real distant." He paused and adjusted the straps of his backpack. "But we all got some counseling and worked things out. And then last summer I went to Indiana."

Just listening to Cody was filling me with all kinds of confused feelings. One second I was identifying with him (and with you, Mystery Baby), and thinking, "Of course he should contact his birthmother." The next second I was relating to Mr. and Mrs. Zeller. I could understand why they might feel a little rejected. I mean, they're the ones who got up in the middle of the night to feed Cody when he was a baby, nursed him through chicken pox, bought him toys and clothes and food.

And then I wondered how I would feel, Em, if you took off to visit Iris someday. Would I be worried you were going to choose her over us, and never come back? At the very least, I'd feel a little jealous, especially if Iris ever has another child and you end up liking your biological sibling better than me.

But then I put myself in Iris's place and everything changed again. After all, your birthmother is the one who gives you life. What could be more important than that? And just because she gives you to someone else to raise doesn't mean she doesn't want you. It just means she isn't ready to be a mother, and she's smart enough to know it. So doesn't she deserve to know how her child is doing, especially if the child himself wants to tell her?

Okay, so then that just proves Iris should be able to come over to our house and visit you anytime she wants, Em. Because after all, if you always know her you won't have to wonder about her, right? And then Mom and Dad (and I) won't have to freak out because you suddenly want to run off and find her.

Cody's voice brought me back to the canyon. "Uh-oh," he said, gazing into the sky.

"What's wrong?" I asked, suddenly panic-stricken. Was a rabid eagle about to dive-bomb us or something?

"See that big black cloud?" Cody said. "I figure we've got about five minutes before we get caught in a downpour."

I pictured us being hit by lightning, washed down

the mountain, and drowned in a flash flood. "How far is it back to the road?" I asked.

"Too far. Anyway, I've got a better idea. Come on."

He took off jogging through the underbrush. This time I kept up with him without complaint. Anything to keep from being drenched.

A few minutes later, we came to the base of a rocky outcropping. Huge boulders, some taller than us, lay piled on top of each other like enormous building blocks. Cody started to climb. I tried to follow, but my sneakers had almost no tread. Fortunately, Cody was able to pull me up after him.

We were scrambling over the third boulder when I heard a clap of thunder. "Just in time," he said, pointing behind him. I looked over his shoulder. We were standing at the mouth of a cave. It was about ten feet wide and almost as tall as I am. I couldn't see how far back it went.

"Are there bats in there?" I asked nervously.

"Not last time I looked," he said. "But there is something amazing inside. Come on."

He walked inside and I followed him. Now I could see that the cave was only about twenty feet deep. That made me feel a little better. I looked up. The roof of the cave was mottled and pockmarked from the wind. To my relief, there were no bats in sight.

Suddenly, there was a flash of lightning and rumble of thunder. An instant later, the skies opened up. I don't think I've ever seen it rain so hard. But then maybe it's just that I've never felt so completely surrounded by the elements. I could hear the wind blowing around the entrance of the cave, see the rain smacking the rocks, and hear the thunder echoing through the canyon. I stood there taking it all in, mesmerized.

"Check this out," Cody said, pointing at the wall of the cave. "I discovered it last time I was hiking here."

I walked over to look. It was a group of crude black-and-red drawings. There was one that looked like a striped snake, and beside it was a black wheel-shaped design and a red stick figure. "Chumash Indian rock art!" I exclaimed, gazing at it with amazement. We had studied it in school, but the only actual example I'd ever seen was on a field trip to Indian Hole, a cave just outside of Laguna Verde that was easily accessible by car. Anyway, it wasn't the same, because at Indian Hole the cave has bars across the entrance to keep out the taggers.

Cody sat cross-legged in front of the drawings. "I like to think of some Chumash guy sitting in here hundreds of years ago, maybe waiting out a storm like we are, drawing this stuff to pass the time."

I sat beside him. Neither of us spoke. We were just imagining. Then after a while Cody began to talk in a quiet voice about the ranch and how important it is to save it from development. And that led into a big conversation about overpopulation, which Cody thinks is the root cause of all the world's problems. Eventually, he pulled out the petition from his backpack and I signed it, and then he told me he'd been trying to write a letter to the newspaper about saving the ranch, but he couldn't seem to get started.

"I'm not much of a writer," he said. "When I look at a blank piece of paper, my brain goes blank, too."

"Maybe I could help you," I suggested. "Tell me the

points you want to make, and I'll try to come up with a first draft."

We were composing the letter in our heads when Cody reached out and touched my leg. At first I thought he was coming on to me and all sorts of conflicting thoughts flashed through my mind. I felt excited, but also confused because it's Marc that I like, plus a little scared because suddenly I realized I was all alone with Cody, miles from the nearest human being, and anything could happen and no one would be around to help me. But at the same time, I felt certain Cody would never do anything out of line.

All those thoughts only took a second to pass through my consciousness, and then I realized Cody was moving his chin ever so slightly toward the mouth of the cave. I turned my head slowly, slowly, and found myself looking at two wet, gray dogs. And then I looked closer at their sharp teeth and wild eyes and realized they were coyotes, and my heart leaped into my throat. At the same moment, they smelled us and froze. Their eyes grew wide, their ears stood up, and then they turned and ran.

Can you believe it, Mystery Baby? Coyotes! I've never been close to a wild animal before, except in the zoo, and these guys must have been no more than ten feet away. Cody said that the rain probably kept them from smelling us until they stepped into the cave. The amazing thing was, I could smell them, too. They smelled like wet dogs, only different. They smelled wild.

Anyway, soon after that, the rain stopped. The ridge was muddy and slippery, so Cody said we should head back to the fire road. I didn't mind, since I was still having that sliding-down-the-mountain fantasy. Anyway, I figured the hike really couldn't have been improved upon at that point. But it turned out I was wrong, because on the way back the sun broke through the clouds and we saw a rainbow. It seemed to stretch across the entire sky, so wide and solid I almost thought we could climb up on it and walk back to Laguna Verde.

Oh, Little Sib, I just realized you don't know what a rainbow is. Or a mountain, or a canyon, or a coyote. I mean, that's obvious, I suppose, because after all, you haven't been born yet. Still, I already think of you as a real person—more real to me sometimes than my own parents are. Or at least easier to talk to.

But just you wait, Em, just you wait. There's a lot to see out here, and I'm going to be your personal tour guide. Which is why I have to help Cody save Howorth Ranch. Because I'm going to take you there. And Mystery Baby, I just know you're going to love it.

November 21

Hey Sib,

It's amazing how fast you can go from total ecstasy to complete misery. Well, not misery exactly, but sort-of-confused unhappiness. In fact, there was only one good thing that happened today, and that was over by eight-thirty. After that, it was all downhill.

I spent most of Sunday working on the letter to the editor. I took the basic information Cody had given me—how big the ranch is, when it was given to the city, stuff like that—and blended it with a firsthand description of our hike. I tried to make the person reading the letter feel like he was actually there, experiencing everything along with us—the view of the canyon, the smell of rain in the air, the rock art, the coyotes' wild eyes, and the endless rainbow. Then I concluded by asking the public to write to the mayor of Laguna Verde and tell him to SAVE THE RANCH!

I took the letter to school on Monday and waited

for Cody at his locker. After he read it, he didn't say a word.

"Okay, you hate it," I said. "No biggie. I'll just start over."

He blinked a few times, as if he were waking up from a dream. "Hate it? Are you kidding? I love it. I'm just amazed that you can write like this. It's like . . . like I'm actually there."

I could feel myself blushing. "This is just a first draft," I pointed out. "You can rewrite it any way you want."

Cody shook his head. "I'm not changing a word. And I want you to put your name on this letter. I'll sign too, but below you. These are your words, and you deserve the credit."

I didn't know what to say. I felt flattered, and really proud. And then I had an idea. The Social Service Committee was meeting after school. So far we hadn't taken on any environmental projects, and I figured Howorth Ranch would be the perfect thing.

Ha, was I ever wrong. But I didn't know that yet. So I invited Cody to come to the meeting, and he said yes.

The committee meets in a conference room next to the library. When I walked in with Cody, Lauren looked at me and raised her eyebrows as if to say, "Well, well, well." And suddenly, I had this horrible feeling she was going to say something about adoption and blow my cover. I mean, I know I'm going to have to tell Cody at some point that my family is adopting a baby, but I want to do it in a positive way, a way that won't make him think that's the only reason I'm hanging out with him. In fact, maybe I'll just lie a teeny bit and pretend my parents decided to adopt *after* I met him, not before.

Anyway, before I could figure out a way to tell Lauren to play dumb, Marc walked in with Noah and Forest. They sat down and Marc looked at Cody. "Hey, what's up?" he asked in a less-than-welcoming voice.

"This is Cody Zeller," I said quickly. "He's involved with a group of people who are trying to save Howorth Ranch from development. I thought it might be a good issue for us to get behind."

Marc looked skeptical. "I don't know about that. We've got a lot on our plate right now—the whole vegetarian food in the cafeteria thing, pushing for a multicultural history course . . . and you want to do this Save The Children thing, right, Sara?"

"Sure," I said, "but we want to get the whole school involved with our projects, don't we? Well, saving the environment is one issue almost everyone can agree on. Remember last year when the P.T.A. planted drought-tolerant shrubs around the school to save water? Even the jocks volunteered to help with that."

"The entire football team has the I.Q. of a shrub," Noah cracked. "It was a perfect match."

Everyone laughed, and then Lauren said, "Let's hear what Cody has to say."

Marc smiled, a little condescendingly I thought, and said, "Go on, Cody. What have you got to say?"

Cody cleared his throat and told us about the ranch. He seemed kind of nervous, cracking his knuckles and tripping over his words—so I helped him out by telling everyone about our hike and how impressed I was by the beauty of the land and the animals.

When we finished, Marc let out a long sigh. Everyone turned to him. "Do you realize," he said, "that when Laguna Verde received state highway improvement funds last year, the city had to promise to build two hundred units of low income housing over the next three years?"

"So?" Forest said with a shrug.

"So Howorth Ranch is the perfect place to build it," Marc said. "The city can put up the two hundred units on the old ranch site and still leave the wilderness areas untouched."

I turned to Cody, who was shaking his head. He didn't seem nervous now. "Once the city council starts carving up the ranch," he said, "there'll be no stopping them. They'll turn one part of it into a housing development, another into a park, and another into a sports complex. The next thing you know, there'll be one tiny strip of wilderness left and the homeowners will be complaining because they're spotting coyotes and mountain lions in their backyard."

"You don't need to convince me about protecting the rights of coyotes and mountain lions," Marc said. "After all, I'm a vegetarian. Are you?"

Cody scowled. "What does that have to do with it?"

I was wondering that myself. This was starting to feel less and less like a discussion and more and more like a fight. It was almost as if Marc were launching a personal attack on Cody. But why? It didn't make sense and it was making me mad.

At the same time, I couldn't help being impressed by how well-informed Marc was on the subject of Howorth Ranch. Cody hadn't mentioned that part of the ranch had been lived on and the rest was wilderness, but Marc knew it anyway.

"The point is," Marc continued, "local government always shortchanges the poor by building low-income housing in industrial areas or next to a freeway. Howorth Ranch is prime real estate and I think it's time some regular people got to enjoy it."

Now Marc was going too far. Without thinking, I cried, "But regular people *can* enjoy it. The ranch is open for everyone to go hiking and camping and rock climbing and—"

"Those are middle-class activities," Marc interrupted. "Working-class people don't care about climbing rocks and picking wildflowers. They just want a roof over their heads."

"Then they'll be much happier in the city where they can walk to the supermarket and the bank," Cody said angrily. "From Howorth Ranch, the nearest shopping center is a thirty-minute car ride away."

Marc countered by calling for a vote. "There are three options," he said. "One: we get actively involved with the Save the Ranch organization. Two: we don't. And three: we shelve it until we have time to do some further research."

Well, naturally everyone except Cody and me voted for option number three. But I had a sneaking suspicion the Social Service Committee wouldn't be discussing Howorth Ranch again, at least not this year.

After the vote, Cody left to talk to his biology teacher about some extra-credit project he was doing. I sat through the rest of the meeting, stewing. I just couldn't understand why Marc had come down on Cody so hard. Sure, some of the stuff Marc said made sense— governments do build low income housing in crummy parts of town. But that doesn't justify turning an ecological gem like Howorth Ranch into a housing development. And it sure doesn't justify treating Cody as if he were some kind of carnivorous cretin.

When the meeting ended, I jumped up to talk to Marc. But he was already walking toward me. "What are you doing hanging around with that eco-dweeb?" he demanded.

"What do you mean?" I said. "Cody's okay."

Marc groaned. "I know his type. They're so busy saving some slimy toad from extinction that they can't see what's really important."

"And what would that be?" I asked.

Marc looked hurt. "If you don't know what I believe in by now," he said, "I'm not going to spell it out for you."

"I thought you cared about people," I said, "but now I'm starting to wonder. I mean, ever since you got appointed chairman of this committee, it's like you're on some kind of egotistical power trip."

"That is so unfair!" Marc cried. He grabbed his backpack and headed for the door.

I ran after him. "Marc, wait," I called. "I'm sorry."

He stopped just outside the door. "I've been meaning to tell you, Sara," he said. He seemed calm now, and very casual. "About that pro-choice concert—I'm not going."

"What? Why not?"

He shrugged. "You want to spend time with the girl who's giving up her baby—what's her name? Iris, right? Well, go ahead."

"But I want you to be there, too," I said.

"If we were going to be alone, that would be one

thing. But this is different." He smiled. "You go hang out with Iris. We'll get together another time."

"But Marc—" I began.

He cut me off with a wave of his hand. "Keep working on that petition about the vegetarian food in the cafeteria. We need more signatures." He slung his backpack over his shoulder. "Later, Sara." Then he walked away.

So what was all that about, Mystery Baby? I mean, was Marc right when he called Cody an eco-dweeb, the kind of person who cares more about bugs than people? Or was Marc just ticked off because someone other than him dared to make a suggestion about what the Social Service Committee should be doing?

Or—and this really blows me away—could it be that Marc is jealous because I went hiking with Cody? That would be stupid because Cody is somebody I just met, whereas Marc and I—well, we've known each other a long time and besides, I thought we were really starting to care about each other. Anyway, Marc and I have so much in common, while Cody, on the other hand, is the kind of guy who likes to get up at the crack of dawn, bicycle to the ocean, catch a few freezing cold waves, and then, just for a little change of pace, jog up a mountain. In other words, not my type.

So why is it I keep thinking about him? Is it because he's adopted? Or is it because I want to look into those blue eyes once more and see the sense of wonder that's shining out of them? Like when we were standing side by side, gazing out over Rattlesnake Canyon. I could feel the love he has for that place, and that made me feel it too.

Oh, I don't know. Maybe it's both those things. All I know for sure is that after I left Marc outside the conference room, I felt confused and just generally crappy inside, and that's why I called Iris. Or was it? Maybe it was what happened later in the evening that made me long to hear her voice. Mystery Baby, you be the judge . . .

It was five o'clock and I was in the ladies' room at the Wharf, changing into one of the hideous hibiscus-flowered mini-dresses that all the waitresses have to wear. As Dad explained when he handed me the dress, one of the waitresses had called in sick, and it was about time I started doing something around the restaurant to earn my allowance.

"So put on this sexist little number and go flirt with that old geezer at Table 10."

Okay, okay, so he didn't actually say that. He didn't have to. I could read between the lines. I straightened my stockings (yes, he makes the waitresses wear stockings), ran a comb through my hair, and pushed open the bathroom door.

Mom was waiting outside to pass judgment. She gazed up and down, nodding her head and proclaiming, "Very pretty. You should dress up more often." Then suddenly, she stopped nodding. "Where did you get that bracelet?" she asked.

It was the beaded leather bracelet Iris had given me. I hesitated, and that's when she remembered seeing one just like it on Iris's wrist. "Did Iris give you hers?" she asked with a disapproving frown.

"No, she made me one just like it," I admitted.

"She makes jewelry?" Mom asked.

I had to laugh. "You don't know anything about Iris, do you?"

Then she got all pissed off and gave me another lecture about how she doesn't want me getting too close to Iris. "Did it ever occur to you that she might not want to tell us every detail of her personal life?" she asked.

"Did it ever occur to you that her child might ask us some questions about his birthmother someday?" I shot back. "What are we supposed to say? 'Oh, we don't know anything about her. After all, we didn't want to get too close.' "

"Yes, it did occur to us," Mom said. "Which is why we're going to ask Iris to put together a scrapbook about herself that we can give to the child when he's older."

Well, fine, Em, but don't you think it would be nice if we could *tell* you a few things about your birthmother, too? And if maybe one day you could even wear the bracelet she made for me? It makes me smile to imagine slipping it onto your wrist someday. Or maybe I should ask Iris to make you one of your own, a little newborn-sized one that we can tie around your wrist together. Now *that* would be cool.

Then Mom ordered me to take the bracelet off while I was working. According to her, "it just doesn't go with the image we're trying to project."

That's right, Mom. Iris's stuff is much too hip, too unique, and too real for this synthetic meat market you call a restaurant.

I pulled off the bracelet, stuck it down my bra (ha—

you should have seen my mother's eyes bug out), and set to work.

So now it's ten-thirty, I'm back home, and Mom and Dad just turned out their light. The restaurant was a nightmare. With every pushy, self-satisfied, overweight old creep I had to wait on, the more exploited and more pissed off and more miserable I felt. Until finally I just had to talk to someone who would understand what I was feeling. And the more I thought about it, the more I knew that person was Iris.

I'm going to wait another few minutes until I hear Dad snoring, then see if I can find Iris's phone number. I don't know what I want to say to her, exactly. It's just the idea of hearing her voice, of making contact with someone who knows what it's like to want to leave home and find your own way. With someone who actually did it.

Ah, good news. I just tiptoed into the hall and heard Dad's tree-shredder snore. Stay tuned, Mystery Baby. I'll let you know what happens . . .

November 22

MYSTERY BABY—

I'm so confused. The phone call didn't turn out the way I'd planned. Not at all. Listen . . .

I waited until Mom and Dad went to bed, then tiptoed out to the kitchen. I found the address book beside the phone, but Iris's number wasn't in it. Then it occurred to me that it might be in the address book my mother carries in her purse.

I found her handbag by the front door and sure enough, there was Iris's number—in pencil, of course, so Mom could erase it after the baby is born and make believe Iris never existed. I took the cordless phone off the base and walked quietly out the back door and across the cold, damp grass. Then I climbed up into the oak tree and dialed Iris's number.

It was ringing. I looked out at the black ocean and the twinkling lights of the off-shore oil platforms and thought about you, Mystery Baby. It's so weird to realize you're in Ellwood with Iris right now—inside her, in fact—but someday you'll be sitting up in the oak tree with me. Only maybe Iris won't be completely out of the picture. In my imagination, the two of us are helping you climb the tree together. It's very symbolic, really—the whole family tree thing, and Iris and me representing the two sides—your birthfamily and your adoptive family.

While I was thinking all that, a voice said, "Hello?"

"Iris. It's Sara."

"Sara?" She sounded worried. "Is something wrong?"

"No, not really," I said. "I'm just sitting up in a tree in our backyard, watching the ocean and thinking about you." I laughed, picturing how weird that must have sounded. "I mean, I just wanted to say hi, that's all."

She laughed, too. "Aren't you cold? It's about forty-five degrees here."

"It's warmer near the ocean. Mostly, I'm thinking about my aching feet. My parents made me work in the restaurant tonight and I think I walked about twenty miles."

"Ugh," she said. "I hate waitressing. I had a job in a truck stop right after I left home. It lasted for exactly one hour. Some guy pinched my ass and I threw a piece of pie in his face. That was the end of my restaurant career."

I cracked up. Then I told her about my evening in the restaurant and she told me about some other horrible jobs she's had. Probably the worst one was the eclair factory. Her job was to squeeze custard into the eclairs, a task which she said was messy, difficult, and mind-numbingly boring. Then one day the machine went berserk and wouldn't shut off, so all the workers started spraying custard at each other and pretty soon it turned into a gigantic food fight—until the boss showed up, turned off the power, and made them stay late to clean everything up.

By the end of the story, I was laughing so hard I couldn't catch my breath. Then she said, "I've had some crummy jobs, but this one I have now is different. For once, I'm doing something important."

"You mean working in the dry cleaners?" I asked uncertainly.

"No. Thanks to your parents, I quit two days ago. I mean making a baby." She laughed softly. "It wasn't a job I applied for, but now that I know this kid is really wanted, it feels good to be bringing him into the—"

Suddenly, I heard a male voice shouting on the other end. Something about where the hell's the beer.

"Okay, babe, I'm coming," Iris called. "I gotta go," she told me.

"One more thing," I said. "About the pro-choice concert in L.A.—are you and Eddie coming?"

She hesitated. "Uh . . . Eddie doesn't want to go."

"Well, neither does Marc. In fact, we had kind of a fight today, all because I went hiking in Howorth Ranch with this guy named—"

There was a shout and the sound of breaking glass. Iris screamed.

"Iris, what happened?" I cried. "Are you all right?"

"Oh, Christ, I gotta go," she muttered.

"What's going on?" I begged. "Did he throw something at you?"

"Calm down, Eddie," I heard her say. "Hey!" she shouted suddenly. "Eddie, don't!"

What was he doing? I pictured him coming toward

her with a broken bottle in his hand. "I'll call the cops," I said. "You get out of there. Are the buses running? You can stay here with—"

"Don't call anyone," Iris snapped. She sounded really pissed. "You hear me, Sara?"

"Did he hurt you?" I asked. "Are you all right?"

"What are you talking about? Look, don't call me again."

"Phone me after he goes to sleep," I said. "Please."

"Thanks for calling, Sara," she answered in a cheerful voice. "I'll see you next month at my doctor's appointment."

Then suddenly, I had an idea. "The concert's this Saturday," I said, talking fast. "Meet me at the Laguna Verde train station at ten o'clock."

No answer.

"Come on. I'm going without Marc. You can go without Eddie. Okay?"

Silence.

"Iris, please. I want to see you. Please?"

I heard a faint click. She had hung up.

I sat there in the tree, trying to ignore the sick churning in my stomach. I didn't know what to do. Part of me wanted to call the cops, despite what Iris had said. But what if I was wrong? What if Eddie wasn't hurting her but I sent the cops out anyway? Iris would never forgive me. Or what if I was right and the cops came, slapped Eddie's hand, and left? He might get twice as mad and beat the crap out of her.

I thought about waking up my parents, but I didn't want to. I knew what their attitude would be. If we call the police on Eddie, will he refuse to sign the relinquishment papers? If we don't call the police, will he hurt the baby? In short, how does this affect *us*?

And then they'd say, "We told you so, Sara," and give me a big lecture about how Iris is the kind of girl who falls for losers, therefore she is a loser, therefore she's not the kind of girl their darling daughter should be spending time with.

I decided not to wake my parents.

Instead, I stayed in the oak tree, thinking, wondering, undecided, confused. I called Iris's number, then hung up before it rang, then dialed again. It rang and rang, but no one answered. I waited half an hour. The temperature was dropping and I was starting to shiver. I called again. No answer.

Finally, I went inside and got into bed with the cordless phone still in my hand. Lying there, staring at the ceiling, I had all sorts of fantasies. In one, I took the bus to Ellwood, knocked down the door of Iris's apartment, and found Eddie beating her. I hit him over the head with a lamp and took Iris home. Only problem with that little picture was that I had no idea where Iris lived. Plus, I doubt I'd have the guts to hit anyone—even a girlfriend abuser—with a lamp.

Eventually, I fell asleep and the fantasies turned into dreams. When I woke up this morning, I called Iris again. Still no answer.

What do I do now?

November 24

Hey Little One,

Today is Thanksgiving, and I have something big to be thankful for. Iris called today. She's okay, or at least my mother said she sounded okay. I didn't talk to her. Mom and Dad wouldn't let me.

Well, that's not exactly true. Actually, I was up in my room when she called and I didn't know it was her on the phone. Mom could have told me—I'm sure she knew I would want to talk to her—but she didn't. It was only later, when I asked who called, that I found out it was Iris.

"How did she sound?" I asked. I'd been calling her repeatedly ever since Monday night, but I'd never gotten an answer. I'd been freaking, but I didn't know what to do.

"Fine," Mom answered. "She apologized for calling us at home instead of going through the lawyer, but she said she just wanted to wish us a happy Thanksgiving."

That may be what she said, but I'm pretty sure she

was calling to let me know she's all right. God, I'm so relieved. I'm not going to call her again—at least not until we've had a chance to talk in person. I think that's what she was trying to tell me with her phone call. I can't talk now, but I'm okay.

But I'm still wondering what really happened that night. Was Eddie attacking her? Why? And will he do it again? I guess I'll have to wait until I see her again to find out the answer. But when will that be? I'm still hoping she'll show up at the train station Saturday, but who knows? If she doesn't, I'll have to wait two weeks until her next doctor's appointment. And with Mom and Dad and Horloff the Horrible breathing down our neck, who knows if we'll have a chance to talk?

Darn. I wish I knew where Iris lives.

Thanksgiving dinner. My grandparents were there—soon to be your grandparents, Em—plus Janie, Bob, and Kenya. Everybody was talking about Iris, about how thankful they are that she's going to let us adopt her baby. But if they're so thankful, why didn't they invite her and Eddie to Thanksgiving dinner?

I know the answer. To them, welcoming a newborn baby into their lives is okay because a baby is sort of a blank slate. You can dump all your hopes and dreams and expectations on him, and mold him—or at least imagine you're molding him—into the person you want. Into a mirror image of yourself.

But once you get to be Iris's age—or my age, for that matter—it's too late. We're individuals, with our own desires, opinions, motivations, ideals. We talk, and demand, and make trouble. Unlike Kenya, we can't be shut up with a bottle or a pacifier. We're real and we're in their faces, and Mom and Dad can't handle that.

Big news. It's eleven o'clock and I just walked into the kitchen to get a piece of Gramma's orange cake. Mom and Dad were there, pigging out on cold, dead turkey flesh.

Then I heard Mom say, "Our birthing class is canceled this Saturday. The instructor went away for Thanksgiving."

"Does Iris know?" Dad asked.

"I heard it from her. She said she's going to L.A. for the day to visit her aunt."

"She has an aunt in L.A.? She never mentioned that."

Mom shrugged. "I just hope she's pro-adoption. I'd die if some relative showed up at the last minute, offering to raise the baby."

I didn't hear any more because I ran back to my bedroom. I'm so excited, I can hardly write. I'm pretty sure Iris doesn't have an aunt in L.A. That was just a code to let me know she's coming to the concert with me. Or at least I hope so.

I gotta call Lauren first thing tomorrow and ask her to cover for me on Saturday. I'll tell Mom and Dad I'm spending the day with her, get them to drop me off at her house, then take a bus to the train station. Oh, Mystery Baby, I can't wait!

November 26

Iris came! I showed up at the train station at ten of ten, paced the platform until ten-fifteen, then gave up and went inside, trying to figure out if I had the nerve—or even the desire—to go to the concert alone. I came back out when I heard them announcing the train. That's when I saw her, getting out of a city bus and jogging heavily across the parking lot.

She's bigger than the last time I saw her. You can really tell she's pregnant now. She looked great, too—her auburn hair was thick and shining, her face was glowing. I called to her and she broke into a smile.

We climbed into the train and grabbed a seat on the ocean side. "You came," I said, feeling elated but a little shy at the same time. I still didn't know Iris all that well. We'd never spent more than an hour together, and now I was going to be with her for an entire day.

"I can't believe we're going to Los Angeles together," she said. "The lawyer said we were only supposed to see each other at doctor appointments and birthing classes."

"You can forget about all that," I told her. "I found out none of those papers you signed mean a thing. You can do whatever you darned well please."

Iris frowned. "But they told me it was for the best. I mean, we're trying to do what's right for the baby. After he's born, I've got to be able to hand him over and get on with my life."

"You have to do what feels right to you," I said emphatically. "Not what my parents or some lawyer tells you." I paused. "You must have wanted to come today, or you wouldn't be here, right?"

Iris nodded. "I had to get out of that apartment. Eddie has got me all confused."

I asked her what had been going on the night I talked to her on the phone. She looked out the window. "Nothing, really," she said. "Eddie got mad and threw a bottle against the wall. We were having a fight."

"A fight about what?" I asked.

She shrugged. "Ever since your parents started paying for my expenses, Eddie has been on my case. He wants me to keep working and give him the money so he can start his own motorcycle shop."

"But that's not fair!" I cried. "You're pregnant. You have to rest and take care of yourself."

"Oh, I don't know," she said, twisting her leather bracelet. "Now that I'm eating better, I feel pretty good. And that shop means so much to Eddie. It's just . . . you know, it doesn't seem right to give away your parents' money to him without their permission."

"It's more than that," I insisted. "That money is for you, to use on yourself." I touched her hand. "I thought you wanted to start making a living selling handmade clothes and jewelry."

"Sure, someday. But I can't do that now."

"Why not?" I asked. "Listen, I've got a plan." I told her my idea about buying a car—or better yet, a van—and taking her jewelry and clothing around to the local craft stores. "Then after the baby's born and you've saved up enough money, you can open your own shop."

Iris looked at me, sort of disbelieving. "You're incredible," she said. "I would never think of something like that."

I asked her why not.

"A million reasons. I haven't made nearly enough jewelry or clothing to think about selling it. Besides, I wouldn't know what to say to the store owners. They probably wouldn't like my stuff any—"

I cut her off right there. "Stop being so negative. All you have to do is sit down and make some stuff. Then buy the van and we'll go around to the stores together."

Iris glanced at me. She looked wary, on edge. "Why are you being so nice to me?"

Why was I? There's just something about Iris that makes me feel drawn to her. I guess it's because there's so much I can learn from her—about leaving home, making it on your own, falling in love, living with a guy. But at the same time, there's so much I can help her with. I mean, if it wasn't for me, she'd be completely under the thumb of my parents, their manipulative lawyer, and Horloff the Horrible. But together, I think we've both got a chance to break free.

Before I could answer, the conductor came around

and we bought our tickets. Iris was smiling like a little kid. "I've never been on a train before," she told me.

That surprised me. It seemed like such a basic thing, one step up from riding in a car. "This is a pretty trip," I told her. "You can see the ocean almost the entire way to L.A."

"Is Los Angeles really as big as they say?" she asked.

Well, turns out she's never been to L.A., either. Man, for someone who's on her own, Iris still has a lot of living to do. "It's huge," I told her. "There's theaters, museums, more stores than you can imagine, freeways everywhere. And people—millions of people. It's awesome!"

The train began to move. Within minutes, the trees thinned out and we were looking at ocean. Iris stared out the window, transfixed. "Don't tell me you've never seen the ocean before," I said.

"Sure I have, but only since I moved to Ellwood. I grew up in the desert, remember? This is still new to me."

That's when I realized I take the ocean pretty much for granted. After all, I've lived within walking distance of the beach my entire life. I closed my eyes and tried to imagine growing up in the desert, mile after mile of sand and scrub and cactus. Then I opened them and gazed out at the shimmering green whitecaps. It was almost as if I were seeing them for the first time. Man, they were beautiful.

"Tell me about the desert," I said. "What was it like growing up there?"

With her eyes still on the ocean, she told me about her family—her welder father who drank too much and then came home in the middle of the night, knocking over furniture and any kids who happened to get in his way; her mother who worked nights as a cleaning lady at an office building and was always tired; her two brothers and four sisters. She was the oldest, and she'd been expected to get all of them ready for school every morning while her mother slept. "I hated school, except for Home Ec. and Art," she said. "That's how I got interested in sewing and jewelry-making."

"What about your friends?" I asked. "What did you do for fun?"

She laughed. "Oh, we were wild! Some of the boys had off-road cycles and ATVs. We used to drink beer and race in the desert every weekend. My boyfriend was a real hell-raiser. He never lost a race."

"Don't you miss him?"

"Sometimes. But I didn't want to spend my life in Indio. Besides, I have Eddie now."

I paused, trying to get up the courage to ask her. "Does he hit you?" I asked at last.

She glared at me, and I was afraid she was going to get up and leave. Then her expression softened. Finally she said, "He has a temper, that's for sure." She shrugged. "He was the first person I met in Ellwood. I was broke, hungry, and I didn't know my way around. Eddie took care of me. Besides, he's the father of my child."

I nodded. Iris hadn't answered my question, not directly anyway. But reading between the lines, I think she was trying to tell me I had overreacted that night on the phone. Okay, so Eddie threw a bottle. That was a stupid thing to do, but it wasn't the same as hitting her. Anyway, what do you expect from an intense, pedal-to-the-metal kind of guy like Eddie? Or Marc, for that matter.

"I know what it's like to fall for someone with a temper," I said. "Marc—he's the guy I was gonna go to the concert with—got mad just because I went hiking with this other guy, Cody." I told her the whole story. "Marc is so full of himself sometimes," I sighed, "but I can't stop thinking about him."

"Still, you came today," Iris pointed out, "even without Marc."

I smiled. "And you showed up without Eddie. Hey, look at that!"

There was a school of dolphins swimming along the shore. Every few seconds one would leap out of the water, then disappear into the waves. Iris stared, absolutely blown away. She'd never seen dolphins before.

The rest of the train ride was a blast. We talked about the kind of clothes and jewelry she should make and where we could sell them. Then we fantasized about the store she'll own someday, and I said I wanted to work in it. Finally, I told her my idea about making a beaded leather bracelet for the baby.

She promised she'd make one, then suddenly she gasped and her eyes grew wide. She put a hand on her stomach. "It's moving," she whispered. "Here, feel."

Iris took my hand and laid it on her stomach. And that's when I felt you kick, Mystery Baby! It was amazing! I mean, I'd already heard your heartbeat and seen a picture of you, but this was something else. This was intense, it was immediate. It was you!

The next thing I knew, the train was pulling into Union Station. The concert was outdoors in Griffith Park, so we asked at the station about which bus to take. The whole way there, Iris stared out the window. She just couldn't get over all the pink mini-malls and the smog and the wide, endless streets jammed with cars.

When we got to the park, we followed the signs to the concert. There were hundreds of people spread out on a big, grassy lawn, all sitting on blankets, talking, and waving signs that said, I'M PRO-CHOICE AND I VOTE. Most of them were in their twenties and very hip-looking, like they'd just walked out of MTV. There was a stage set up at the far end of the crowd, covered with amplifiers, microphones, and wires. A banner above the stage said PRO-CHOICE COALITION.

Iris and I paid at the booth—it was a free concert, but they were asking for donations—and walked across the grass. I noticed people following Iris with their eyes. Some did a double take. I guess it was like Marc had said—they were surprised to see a pregnant woman at a pro-choice event. But hey, the point is to give people a choice, right? What you decide is up to you.

We found an empty patch of grass and sat down. Pretty soon the first band took the stage. Their name was Craze and they played a really radical mixture of hard-edged rock and political rap. I thought they were awesome, but when I asked Iris what she thought, she looked kind of stunned. It turns out practically the only music she's ever listened to is country, plus some mainstream rock and roll.

"I don't think I belong here," she said. "These people are all college kids, kids with money. They're smart, they've been around. They understand this kind of music. I don't."

"You're smart, too," I said firmly, "and you've been around plenty. Just open your mind and listen. That's all there is to it."

The next group was called Nolina. They played all acoustic songs, kind of sad and bluesy and dark. Iris was getting into it, I could tell. At one point, she closed her eyes and swayed along with the music. I smiled, thinking about you, Little Sib. Could you hear the music, too? Were you swaying and rolling inside your sack of fluid, all loose-limbed and happy, like those dolphins we saw playing in the waves?

During the break, we checked out the booths on the edge of the lawn. Some were raising money for political groups. PETA was there, Planned Parenthood, Greenpeace, stuff like that. There were food booths, too, with people selling everything from hot dogs to hummus. I convinced Iris to try a tofu taco, and guess what? She liked it. I told her I'd lend her one of my vegetarian cookbooks next time I see her. Who knows, Em? I might turn your birthmom into a vegetarian yet.

While we ate, we wandered by the craft booths. They were selling tie-dyed vests, T-shirts, jewelry, hats, and sandals. "You should be selling your stuff here," I said. "You could clean up."

"You never answered my question," Iris said. "Why are you being so nice to me?"

"Because you're the birthmother of my soon-to-be baby sister, and that makes us family. Because I care about you. Because . . . I don't know. We're from different worlds, but it's like we're soul mates. I knew it that first day I met you."

Iris just smiled. "We don't know for sure the baby is a girl," she said softly. "We could be surprised."

I shook my head. "No way. I've got a feeling about this. Just wait and see."

The next band—an all-woman group called Taurus Rising—was about to begin. But as the first guitar chord blasted through the loudspeakers, a scuffling sound came from behind us.

I spun around to see a crowd of anti-abortion protesters marching toward us. They held their ABORTION IS MURDER signs above their heads like crosses.

A few pro-choice people jumped to their feet. "Go home!" someone shouted. "You're not welcome here!"

"Murderers!" One of the anti-abortion people cried. "You should be ashamed of yourselves."

Up on the stage, the band was still playing. The anti-abortion protesters began marching through the middle of the crowd. Then one of them, a thin middle-aged woman who was carrying rubber baby dolls in each hand, spotted Iris.

"You don't belong with these killers," she called, thrusting her dolls in Iris's face. "Stand up and march with us!"

Everyone around us turned to stare at Iris. She looked down at the grass, obviously embarrassed and uncomfortable.

A muscular man with a ponytail jumped up behind us. "Leave her alone, you lunatic!" he cried. He snatched one of the baby dolls from the woman's hand and threw it into the crowd.

The thin woman jumped at him, clawing at his face. Iris struggled to her feet and scrambled out of the way. I leaped up and joined her. A few of the nearby anti-abortion protesters ran over and began kicking the man. His pro-choice friends jumped to their feet and attacked the pro-lifers.

The band had finally stopped playing. All around us, people were yelling and fighting. Then someone on the stage grabbed a microphone and shouted, "Media alert!"

I looked up to see a TV news van bouncing across the field. It stopped and a man with a video camera on his shoulder jumped out and began filming the crowd. I looked back to see a woman with an ABORTION IS MURDER sign bump into Iris, almost knocking her over.

"Sara, we have to get out of here," Iris said, grabbing my arm. Her eyes were wide and frightened.

I was frightened, too. What if we ended up on the evening news and my parents happened to tune in? I'd probably be grounded until Iris's baby graduated from college.

"Follow me," I told Iris. I began pushing my way through the noisy, churning crowd, past pro-choicers and pro-lifers, stepping over broken protest signs and scattered picnic lunches. Iris walked behind me, one hand clutching the back of my jacket and the other wrapped protectively around her belly.

We were near the edge of the crowd when someone shoved me hard from the side. I fell to the grass, taking Iris with me. When I looked up I saw a reporter, microphone in hand, heading our way.

"Get up!" I shouted at Iris. I grabbed her hand and pulled her to her feet. Still holding hands, we broke away from the crowd and ran across the park. In the distance, a police siren whined.

We didn't stop running until we were back at the

bus stop. "Oh my God, that was insane!" I cried. Now that it was over, I felt exhilarated, almost giddy. I started to laugh.

Iris wasn't even smiling. "I shouldn't have come," she said unhappily. "What if the baby had been hurt? I never could have lived with myself."

Man, I felt like such a butthead. Iris had been worrying about you, Mystery Baby, but all I'd been able to think about was getting into trouble with my parents. I felt like kicking myself.

I told Iris what I was feeling, but instead of criticizing me or laughing it off, she just stared at me. "Your parents don't know we're here?" she asked at last.

"I told you that," I said, although I realize now that I didn't put it in those exact words. Maybe because I was afraid Iris wouldn't come if she knew. "But it doesn't matter," I added quickly. "Like I told you, those papers you signed don't mean a thing. You can do whatever you want. And so can I, for that matter."

"But I don't want to have to lie to your parents," she said.

"You don't have to lie. All you have to do is not tell them." I paused, suddenly worried. "You won't, will you?"

Iris smiled. "No. I don't want to get you in trouble. Besides, I had a good time—until the lady with the rubber dolls showed up, anyway."

I giggled. "It was kind of exciting though, wasn't it? There was so much energy flowing through the crowd, so much passion." A bus was rumbling toward us, but I didn't feel like leaving. Not yet. "Come on," I said, touching Iris's arm. "Let's go for a walk."

We spent the next couple of hours walking through

the park, eating ice-cream bars, sitting in the sun, watching the children fly kites. Then we caught the bus back to Union Station and took the next train home.

When I left Iris at the Laguna Verde train station, I made her promise she would use some of the money my parents had given her to buy a van. "Then call me," I said, "and we'll figure out a game plan for selling your stuff."

Iris nodded. She turned to leave, then turned back. "I guess I knew all along you weren't going to tell your parents where you were going today. Or who you were going with. But I came anyway."

"I'm glad you did," I said.

She grinned. "Me, too." Then she turned and ran across the parking lot to catch the Ellwood bus.

December 6

Dear Sis,

I woke up today to the sound of the phone ringing. A few seconds later I heard my mother call, "Sara, it's for you." I squinted at the clock. It was seven-fifteen on a school day. Who would be calling me now? My first thought was Iris. But why would she be calling me at that hour?

I got up and dragged myself to the kitchen phone. Turns out it was Cody, and he had big news. "Have you seen this morning's paper?" he asked.

"Are you kidding?" I laughed. "I haven't even seen daylight yet."

"Well, check out the editorial page and call me back," he said. Then he hung up.

I ran out to the driveway. The concrete was so cold it made my feet ache. I turned to the editorial page, but our letter wasn't there. I had long ago given up hope of seeing it, figuring the conservative *Times-Register* was all in favor of developing Howorth Ranch.

Then I spotted an article on the facing page under

the heading "Local Voices." It was my Letter To The Editor, only the paper had printed it as an editorial! I ran back to the kitchen, looked up Cody's number, and dialed.

"This is incredible!" I cried when he answered. "What do you suppose made them want to run the letter as an editorial?"

"Because it's thoughtful and articulate," he replied. "At least, that's what the editor told me."

Well, it turns out the editor tried to call me last week, but no one was home. So she called Cody, and he gave her permission to turn the letter into an editorial. "I wanted to surprise you," he told me.

"Well, you succeeded," I said with a laugh.

"This is going to be great publicity for the Save the Ranch movement," he said. "I sure am glad I took you there. I never could have written anything like this myself."

I wondered if that was the only reason he'd asked me to go hiking with him—to convince me to write a Letter To The Editor about Howorth Ranch. If it's true, I guess I can't really complain. After all, the only reason I agreed to the hike was so I could pick his brains about what it's like to be adopted.

I hung up the phone feeling confused and a little sad. I mean, sure, maybe I'd used Cody a little—at first, anyway. But after our hike together, I'd felt really close to him. And I was hoping he felt the same way toward me.

Forget it, Sara, I told myself. He's an eco-dweeb, just like Marc said.

Marc. I was still thinking about him. We hadn't talked privately since our fight. Oh, he was friendly enough toward me, but whenever we had a chance to be alone, he seemed to disappear.

I decided to take the newspaper to school and show him my editorial. I had an idea that I thought might interest him. An idea that would help us make up.

Mom and Dad saw the Save the Ranch editorial and liked it. They even said they were proud of me. It felt good to hear my parents praising me for a change, but there was something about their delight that bothered me. Why were they tickled pink when I spoke out about Howorth Ranch, but outraged at the thought of me attending a pro-choice concert? I decided to ask them.

"The difference between the two is obvious," my father said, sitting down at the dining room table to sip his morning coffee. "Didn't you see the photo in the newspaper? The pro-life people showed up and there was a big scuffle, just like I predicted."

"Six people were arrested," my mother chimed in. "Dozens were injured. One of them could have been you."

"So what?" I cried. "The civil rights movement never would have succeeded if people hadn't been willing to get arrested or even killed for what they believe. in. Neither would the anti-war movement, or—"

"When you're eighteen, you can do as you please, Sara," my father said. "But until then, please confine your protests to the printed page."

Amazing how my parents can toy with my mind. Before breakfast began, I'd been feeling good about that editorial. Now I felt like setting the newspaper on fire and tossing it in the middle of the dining room table.

Instead, I grabbed it and walked out the door, eager to get to school and talk to Marc.

I found him in front of the school, corralling kids and convincing them to sign our petition demanding vegetarian entrees in the cafeteria. He was good at it, too. In the five minutes I stood there watching him, he gathered three signatures. I had to hand it to Marc. It took me about two hours to get that many kids to sign.

When Marc saw me, he tucked his petition under his arm and walked over. "We're up to eighty-four names," he announced. "I figure we'll stage one more protest demonstration, then march into Saldano's office and present our demands. I think she'll listen, especially now that we've got the power of the Social Service Committee behind us."

"We *are* the Social Service Committee," I pointed out.

He grinned. "Exactly."

"Did you see the paper this morning?" I handed him the editorial page and pointed to my article.

He skimmed it and smiled. "So you and Mr. Save The Slugs have joined forces. Very nice."

"That's not the point," I said. "What's important is that the newspaper liked my letter enough to turn it into a 'Local Voices' editorial."

Marc shrugged. "You're a good writer, Sara. I always knew that."

"Don't you get it?" I said. "This is a source of publicity we never considered before. Let's sit down together and write a letter about our struggle to get vegetarian food in the cafeteria. Maybe we could work on it after—"

"Reality check, Sara," Marc said, knocking on my skull. "Half the ads in the *Times-Register* are for restaurants like that meat market your parents own. Fat chance they're going to print a letter about vegetarians."

"But the paper prints lots of articles about the high school," I pointed out.

"Sure, fluff about the football team and who made the honor roll. Anyway, writing for the *Times-Register* is just buying into the corporate media monopoly."

Marc gets me so confused sometimes. I was trying to help our cause, but he made it sound like my idea was totally lame. Like I was being co-opted by the conservative honchos at the *Times-Register* but was too dumb to know it.

"Hey, don't look so down," Marc said, reaching out to lift my chin until I was looking him in the eye. "I say we circumvent the mainstream media entirely and create an underground alternative to the school paper, something really satirical and subversive—with you as the editor, of course."

I felt the warmth of his fingers against my chin. His eyes seemed to burn into mine, turning my brain to cottage cheese. "An underground paper?" I repeated. "Do you really think we could pull it off?"

"First things first," he said, dropping his hand. "I'm planning a protest demonstration during lunchtime next week. If that doesn't convince the school to listen to our demands, then we'll think about trying other tactics."

He handed back my copy of the *Times-Register* and

walked off to collect more signatures. It was only then that I realized the pro-choice concert had happened over a week ago and Marc still hadn't asked me anything about it—if I'd gone, if I'd enjoyed myself, if I'd been caught in the fighting. Nothing.

Thanks a lot, Marc. You may be a smart, savvy idealist with enough charisma to start a wildfire, but sometimes you're a total ass.

December 9

Hi Kiddo!

Iris called this afternoon, and guess what? She bought a van! Mom and Dad were at the restaurant when she called, so I told her to drive over and show it to me.

She arrived about an hour later in an ancient, avocado-green Chevy van. The body is rusted, the upholstery is ripped, and the exhaust pipe is falling off, but hey, it runs and that's what counts, right?

Then I invited Iris inside. She was a little hesitant at first—she felt funny about being there without my parents' permission—but then I reminded her that it's my house too, and she loosened up. Besides, she had to use the bathroom.

I showed her around, then we went into the kitchen and I made her a veggie burger. She kept oohing and aahing about the deck and the hot tub and the view of the ocean from the loft above my parents' bedroom. I guess compared to the house she grew up in, our place is pretty luxurious. Personally, I'd be just as happy living in a cruddy one-bedroom apartment, as long as it was all mine.

"This is a great house for a kid to grow up in," Iris said between bites of veggie burger. (She said it tasted pretty good, considering it was made out of plants.)

I thought back to when I was a little kid. I'd had a blast bobbing for Halloween apples in the hot tub, sending my remote-controlled car sailing off the edge of the deck, and playing pirates up in the oak tree. Of course, it wasn't the real world. It was the sanitized, all-white, no-poor-folks-allowed Laguna Verde version, but back then it was all I knew.

I took Iris out back and showed her the oak tree. Then I told her how at first I'd felt a little jealous about sharing it—and my life—with a new baby. "But now I can't wait to teach my little sister how to climb this tree," I said. "In fact, I'm hoping we can teach her together."

Iris frowned. "I don't think your parents are going to go for that."

"But what about you?" I asked. "What do you want?"

Iris gazed out across the lawn. "All I can think about is bringing this baby into the world," she said at last. "After that, everything is blank. I just can't picture it."

"I can," I said. "You'll be selling your clothing and jewelry all over Laguna Verde. Maybe even opening your own store. Then you and Eddie can get an apartment here in town."

She laughed. "I can't see Eddie living in Laguna Verde."

I shrugged. "Whatever. The main thing is you and I will still be friends. We can take the baby to the beach, hang out in L.A. And you can teach me how to ride a motorcycle."

Just as Iris opened her mouth to answer, the back door flew open and Mom and Dad walked out on the deck. Behind them were Janie, Bob, and Kenya. I stood and stared. What were they doing here? Then I remembered. They'd told me at the beginning of the week that they were taking off Friday evening to have dinner with Janie and Bob.

Mom and Dad walked to the edge of the deck and squinted into the twilight. Then their eyes grew wide.

"Iris!" my mother called. "Is that you?"

"Yes," she said anxiously, hurrying toward them. "I just—I came to show you my new van."

My parents stepped off the deck and walked across the lawn to meet us. "That van in the driveway is yours?" my father asked. He frowned. "It looks like it needs a lot of work."

"Just body work, mostly," Iris said. "It runs great, and it was cheap."

"Anyhow," I added, "she needs it to drive around to local craft stores and sell her clothing and jewelry."

"You make jewelry?" Janie asked from the edge of the deck.

"Iris," my mother said, "these are our friends Janie and Bob, and their adopted son, Kenya."

Everyone exchanged hellos and my father said, "Let's go into the living room. It's getting chilly out here."

We trooped into the living room and sat down. Iris couldn't take her eyes off Kenya, who was cooing and drooling in Bob's arms. "Your son is adopted?" she asked him.

"That's right," Bob replied. "I think you know his birthmother—Megan Stolinski."

Iris looked amazed. "He's Megan's kid? Man, that's so weird!"

"Is Megan a friend of yours?" I asked.

Iris shook her head. "I've never even met her. We just talked on the phone a couple of times. A friend told me to call her because I was pregnant and I didn't know what I wanted to do. My friend said Megan had given her baby to some people in Laguna Verde to adopt and maybe I could do that, too."

"After you talked to Megan, she called me," Janie explained, "and I called Marty and Jeanette."

"We owe Megan a big thank you," I said. "If it wasn't for her, we wouldn't all be sitting here right now."

My father shot me a look that made it clear he didn't want to be sitting here right now—not if Iris was part of the gathering. I ignored him.

"Iris, I was just about to make dinner," my mother said stiffly. "Would you like to join us?"

"Oh, no thanks," she began. "I—"

"Come on, stay," I urged. I knew my parents were squirming, and I was enjoying every minute of it. Besides, I figured that if Iris really did stay, everything would turn out fine and my parents would see the world wasn't about to end just because she stepped inside our house.

Bob and Janie were smiling encouragingly. Mom said, "Please, Iris, we'd love to have you."

"Well—" Iris whispered.

"Good, it's settled," I said. I turned to Janie and Bob. "What's Megan doing now?"

"She's back in high school," Janie replied. "She'll be going to the junior college in Ellwood next year."

"Sara," my mother broke in, "I need you to help me in the kitchen, please."

Oh, great. I knew my mom just wanted to get me alone so she could chew my head off. I trudged into the kitchen. Sure enough, Mom was standing there with her hands folded across her chest. "Just what are you trying to do, young lady?" she demanded.

"What do you mean?" I asked.

"What were you and Iris doing in the backyard together?"

"Shooting heroin. Why?"

Mom did a slow burn.

"Come on, lighten up," I laughed. "Iris came over to show off her new van, just like she said. What was I supposed to do? Leave her standing on the front porch?"

"I don't feel comfortable seeing Iris socially," Mom said. "It's just going to make it harder to go our separate ways after the birth."

"So why do we have to?" I asked.

Mom took a pot out of the cupboard, too worked up to stand still. "I need to know this baby is mine. I don't think I can do that if I'm worried Iris is going to be popping over at any moment."

It was the same old line Mom and Dad had been handing me from the beginning, but I didn't buy it. "You act like you don't want Iris involved at all," I said. "Like you wish you could just go down to the corner and buy a baby out of a vending machine."

Mom looked ready to explode. But before she could say anything, Janie breezed into the kitchen. "I know you're about to have a nervous breakdown," she said, throwing her arm around my mother, "but you did the right thing. Bob and I had Megan over a couple of times before the birth and everything went fine."

"I just like to be prepared for things," my mother said in a shaky voice. "I don't like surprises."

Yeah, because being surprised means you can't be in control. And that means you can't be the boss, right, Mom?

"Relax, Jeanette," Janie said soothingly. She turned to me. "Sara, you go back out. I'll help your mother get dinner ready."

What a relief! I hurried back to the living room to find that Bob had handed Kenya over to Iris. She was smiling down at the baby's tiny brown face, totally enthralled. I glanced at my father. He looked like a man in the throes of terminal heartburn.

Okay, Mystery Baby, I admit it. I enjoyed seeing my parents being forced to cope with something they couldn't control. I mean, what were they going to do—send Iris to her room? Ground her? Nope. They just had to accept her as a free-willed human being and deal with it. Something they refuse to do with me.

Finally, it was time for dinner. Mom made pasta primavera (at last—something without meat!), and it was good. While we ate, Janie asked Iris about her sewing and her jewelry-making. I showed off the beaded leather bracelet Iris made me, and Iris showed us her purse, a colorful shoulder bag with a knotted fringe, which she'd designed and made herself.

Then we got into a big conversation about Iris's future. She told everyone how she was hoping to sell her crafts to local stores and eventually open a store of her own. So of course my father gave her this long, boring lecture about how she should really go back to school and study design or jewelry-making—and definitely business.

"Too many people try to open stores without knowing the first thing about running a business," he said.

"That's why you see the stores come and go so fast downtown," my mother agreed. "People have the merchandise, but they don't know how to market it. They don't know how to hire the help, or keep records, or buy advertising."

Iris was hanging on every word, but I wasn't impressed. Sure, planning a project is fine—in moderation. But what's wrong with learning by doing? If Mom and Dad had their way, there would be so much studying and planning and estimating and projecting that no one would ever get it together to do anything. It's like this chain of restaurants they want to open up and down the coast. They've been talking about it for years. If they want it so much, why don't they just take a chance and do it?

After dinner, we went back into the living room for coffee. The tense vibes my parents were putting out hung in the air like heavy humidity. Iris felt them, there was no doubt about that.

"I have to get home," she said. "Eddie's expecting me. Can I use your bathroom?"

My mother pointed out the way and Iris disappeared down the hallway.

"See? That wasn't so bad," Janie said with a reassuring smile.

My mother managed to smile back. "It wasn't, was it?"

"Iris is a nice girl," Bob said. "She's got talent, too. If she has the motivation to finish school, she could really go somewhere with her clothing designs."

"The first thing she needs to do is get away from that boyfriend of hers," my father said. "He's trouble."

"That's not true," I shot back. "Eddie loves Iris."

"Oh? And how would you know that?" he asked.

"She told me. He doesn't abuse her, either. I don't know where you got that idea."

"Megan told me," Janie broke in. "I assumed Iris had told her."

I knew that couldn't be true. Iris had told me Eddie didn't hit her, and I know she wouldn't lie to me. I didn't bother arguing about it though, because the adults had moved on to another subject—something about my mother's pasta primavera.

After a while, I began to notice that Iris had been gone an awfully long time. Suddenly, I had this image of her sitting in the bathroom crying because my mother and father had made her feel so unwelcome. Without a word, I got up and walked down the hall to find her. Mom called after me, but I ignored her.

I found Iris in your room, Em. I had showed it to her before, but she hadn't done more than glance at it. Now, however, she was standing in front of the crib, gazing at the moon-and-stars mobile that hung over it. When I called her name, she spun around. There were tears in her eyes.

"What's wrong?" I asked.

She shook her head. "Nothing. It's stupid."

"No. Tell me."

Iris smiled. "This room is so beautiful. It's so much more than I could ever give a kid."

For the first time since Iris had arrived, I wondered if maybe I shouldn't have invited her. What if seeing our house had made her feel like her house wasn't good enough? And what if seeing the baby's room and knowing that her child would be living there made her feel she wasn't good enough?

"You've got love, haven't you?" I said. "That's all you really need to give a kid. That's what matters."

"I guess," she said. "But this kid is going to have love and a whole lot more. He—"

"She," I broke in.

Iris laughed. "She's going to have an incredible life. I'm really happy for her. It just makes me wish I could be adopted."

"You already have been. By me." I held out my arms. "Come here, Sis."

Iris made a face like "oh, get serious," but she stepped forward anyway and let me hug her. And then she hugged me back. A second later, my mother walked into the room.

"Is everything all right?" she asked. She was so anxious she looked like she was about to leap out of her skin.

"Yeah," Iris said, stepping away from me. "Everything's fine. I was just looking at the baby's room and thinking what a great life you're going to give him. I know you and your husband are going to be wonderful parents."

Mom looked all pleased and flustered and self-conscious. Unlike me, she didn't make any attempt to hug Iris. She just stood there, smiling and saying, "I'm very happy to hear you say that, Iris. Very happy."

And that was that. Iris drove away in her new van.

I went to my room and read a book. Mom and Dad stayed in the living room and watched a video with Janie and Bob. But this morning I overheard Mom and Dad talking in the kitchen.

"It went much better than I expected," I heard Dad say. "I'll admit that."

"It made me happy to hear Iris say she thinks we'll make wonderful parents for her baby," Mom said.

"Yes, it was probably good for her to see the baby's room," Dad said. "I'm sure it makes the whole thing more real to her."

Mom: "You know, maybe Sara did us a favor by asking Iris into the house."

Dad: "Don't tell her that, or she'll go and do just the opposite."

"Oh, Marty," my mother said. Then they both laughed.

Normally my father's know-it-all attitude would piss me off, but in fact I feel terrific. Because my parents found out that having Iris around is a positive thing. Because now they'll be that much less freaked-out when I ask her over again. And because for once in my life they realized that they were wrong and—deal with it, folks—I was right.

December 15

Hi, Little One! Sorry it's been so long between letters, but I've been so busy, I haven't had a chance to write. Even now, I'm scribbling this in the school cafeteria between bites of cottage cheese and fruit salad, so pardon the peach juice stains.

Marc postponed our protest demonstration until next week so he could devote full attention to his midterms. I'm not complaining. Christmas vacation starts next Wednesday, and between now and then I've got two tests to take and one paper to write. What with school and everything else that's happened, I'm stressed to the max. Not that it's been all bad.

For one thing, our dinner with Iris really seems to have made a difference. A week has passed since she was here, and already I've talked to her on the telephone three times and seen her twice without having to lie to my parents. Okay, so the truth is I didn't mention the phone calls to them, and the two times I saw Iris were at her doctor's appointment and her birthing class—in other words, nothing the lawyer wouldn't approve of. But hey, no one objected when I suggested we all go out for ice cream after leaving Horloff the Horrible's office, and my mother actually invited me to the birthing class. Of course, she went back to her old anal-retentive self after what happened during the class—but that comes later.

About the phone calls . . . mostly I've been giving Iris pep talks, trying to convince her to get to work on her clothing designs and jewelry-making. You see, after my parents' downer lecture about how she should go back to school, she's been practically paralyzed with self-doubt.

"I don't think I'm ready to sell my stuff to local stores," she told me about a dozen times. "It's like your parents said—I need to learn more about design and business. I don't know what I'm doing."

"Stop listening to them," I told her. "Their entire lives can be summed up in one simple phrase—play it safe. Do you know that Thomas Edison only had three months of formal schooling? Good thing he didn't have my mother and father for parents. We'd still be using candles and kerosene lanterns."

I guess I finally got through to her because when I saw her at the birthing class, she told me she was making some earrings out of beads and safety pins, and working on a design for a patchwork vest.

Okay, the birthing class. It was bizarre, to say the least. I mean, there were six other pregnant women there, and they were all about thirty years old, WASPy, and well-to-do. Iris was the only teenager, the only unwed mother, the only one choosing adoption, and the only one who didn't have her husband with her.

Looking around the room at the well-groomed women sitting on big pillows on the floor, leaning against their husbands, I felt for Iris. It's not as if everyone wasn't nice to her—in fact, the other women went out of their way to be sugary sweet—it's just that they so obviously viewed her as different from them. Different and disadvantaged and someone to be pitied.

"Don't tell me you didn't screw around when you were Iris's age," I felt like saying. "Only difference was, you could afford birth control. Or if that didn't work, a quickie abortion between semesters, then back to college in time for your first class."

But I didn't say it. Instead, I turned to Iris and said, "How's Eddie?"

"Okay. Fine."

"I'm dying to meet him. Why don't you bring him over for dinner sometime?"

I saw my mother tense, but Iris didn't seem to notice. "He doesn't want to be involved in the adoption," she said. "He told me he's never going to see the baby, so what does it matter? He'd rather pretend it just doesn't exist."

"But he could see the baby if he wanted," I said. "I mean, some adoptive families maintain a lot of contact with the birthparents after the birth. I read that in a book about open adoption."

Now my mother was doing a lot more than tensing. She was practically convulsing. I guess she didn't realize I'd actually been reading those books she'd given me a few weeks ago, or that not every page of them spews forth the party line Mom and Dad have been handing me.

But before she could say anything, the birthing instructor, a plump, Earth-Mother-type with mounds of curly black hair, smiled and said, "Welcome, everyone. Tonight we're going to work on our breathing and relaxation exercises. Then we'll watch a video of an actual birth."

We spent the next half hour massaging Iris while she lay on the floor, straddled a birthing chair (kind of like a big toilet), and stood hanging onto something that looked like a coatrack with armrests. The whole while, the three of us were panting like idiots and shouting "Hoo hoo, hee!" until we felt like we were going to faint.

Supposedly, the panting and shouting helps the pregnant woman to relax and focus, but it was hard to believe it wasn't just a big practical joke invented by the class instructor. I mean, picture, if you can, an entire room of yuppie couples (and us) hooing and heeing at top volume. Every now and then Iris and I would look at each other and just start giggling. Then Mom would smile indulgently and say, "Take it from someone who's been there—it helps," and we'd start again.

Then came the birthing movie. I was expecting more silly panting and massaging, but what I got was a first-class ticket on an emotional roller coaster. I mean, giving birth is intense, Em. For starters, it hurts a lot more than I ever realized. The woman in this video was groaning, her face contorted in pain, sweat running down her neck and onto her breasts. Her husband was holding her, encouraging her, letting her squeeze his fingers until I thought they would break.

It went on and on like that, the contractions getting longer, the woman's groans escalating to screams, until suddenly an off-camera voice announced, "I can see the head." Then the camera panned down to the woman's crotch and I learned that when you're giving birth, you can forget about modesty. I mean, this woman was hanging out there for all the world to see. And the amazing thing was, she was too wrapped up in the moment to even care.

And then suddenly, it happened. A real, live, human head popped out between the woman's legs, and the next thing I knew, the whole baby slid out, coated in blood and goop. Now the mom and dad were crying and laughing, just completely exhausted and exhilarated. And then there was a tiny, wavering cry as the baby took its first breath. A new life had begun.

When the video ended and the lights came on, everyone in the room had tears in their eyes. Including Iris. Including Mom and me. Slowly, we got up and stumbled out into the sunshine.

That's when Iris burst out sobbing.

"Are you all right?" my mother asked, her hands reaching toward Iris but not quite touching her. The other couples glanced at us, then looked quickly away and hurried to their cars.

Iris didn't even notice. She shook her head, tears streaming down her face. "I didn't think . . . I didn't know it would be so hard," she gasped.

"Childbirth is quite an ordeal," my mother said. "But we'll be there for you. I know you'll do fine."

Iris smiled weakly through her tears, but I knew it wasn't the physical pain she was worried about. It was the thought of going through the entire process of bringing a new life into the world—the pain, the blood, the fear, the joy—only to hand the baby over to someone else. That's what was breaking Iris's heart. But Mom didn't seem to see that.

"Iris," I said, "you have to do what makes you happy."

"But I can't keep the baby," she said. "It wouldn't be fair to her. I want this kid to have the fancy crib, the toys, the big backyard. I want her to have two grown-up parents and a cool big sister. It's what I wish I had. How could I refuse it for her?"

"You're doing a brave thing," my mother said, finally catching on. "A good thing. There'll be sad moments, but in time you'll know you made the right choice."

Iris nodded, but I wasn't sure she believed it. She wiped her eyes, then turned and hurried to her van.

"Wait!" I called. "I'll come with you."

But Iris shook her head. "I'm okay. Really." She started the van and drove off.

I turned back to Mom. She looked angry and I couldn't figure out why. Then she said, "I wish you'd stop putting crazy ideas into her head. If this adoption falls apart, we'll know who to blame."

I couldn't believe my ears. "What are you talking about?" I cried.

"All that foolishness about visiting the baby after it's born, and suggesting that Eddie visit, too. You're just confusing her."

"I'm giving her options, that's all," I shot back. "Anyway, I'm just repeating what I read in one of your books. Some birthmothers stay in close contact with their babies even after the adoption. Some even help to raise the child."

"Sara, let's get one thing straight," my mother said firmly. "I don't care how other people have chosen to live their lives. All I know is what's right for me. I simply will not have Iris co-parenting our baby. Either we're raising this child ourselves—or we won't be raising him at all."

Mom sounded so sure of herself, I was starting to waffle. Was I wrong to think that Iris deserved a chance to watch her baby grow up? And what about you, Mystery Baby? Was it possible for you to really, truly feel good about yourself, knowing that your birthmother had relinquished her right to be your parent, had handed over your upbringing to someone else, had never even made an effort to see you again?

It was then that I knew I had to talk to Cody. Aside from baby Kenya, he was my only real-life connection to the world of adopted kids. If anyone could tell me what it felt like to grow up without a birthmother, it was him.

"Mom, I'm not driving home with you," I said.

"What? Why not?"

"There's someone I need to talk to. It's not Iris, so don't stress. I'll be back by dinnertime."

I expected Mom to forbid me to go, to order me into the car. But she didn't. She just nodded, a little sadly, I thought. Does that mean she finally understands that I'm an individual with my own agenda? Or has she just given up on me? I don't know.

I turned and walked off to call Cody.

December 16

DEAR SIB,

I'm up early to study, but I can't concentrate because I want to tell you about what happened with Cody. I can still hear his voice and see his blue eyes and blond eyelashes sprinkled with sand, still feel his hands on my hips as he—

Hang on. I'm getting ahead of myself. Let me take a deep breath and start from the beginning . . .

When I got off the bus at Stony Beach, the sun was hot, but the wind that was blowing off the sand was crisp and cool. The ocean was clear and green and the waves were rolling in, throwing up foam as they hit the rocks.

I walked across the sand. A couple of kids were flying kites, a few people were walking their dogs, but most of the people on the beach were surfers. One of them was Cody.

"Hi," I called, walking up. He was kneeling in the sand, rubbing wax on his surfboard. His wetsuit and towel lay nearby. "How's the surf?"

He looked up and grinned. "Four feet and hollow." He tossed the stick of wax on his board and sat down in the sand. "I'm glad you called when you did. I was just about to leave the house. What's up?"

What could I say? I still hadn't told him about Iris. I considered telling him now, but it just seemed too weird. I mean, how could I explain why I hadn't bothered to mention until now that our family was adopting a baby? And what if he decided I was only interested in him because he was adopted? He'd probably get pissed and refuse to talk to me. I couldn't handle that—especially not now, when I needed his perspective so much.

"I just wanted to see you again," I said at last. It was true, too. Again and again I'd found myself daydreaming about the time we'd spent together in the cave at Howorth Ranch. Just the memory of it made me feel relaxed and peaceful.

"No kidding?" he said. "I wanted to see you too, but I asked your friend Lauren what was up with you and that Marc dude and she told me you were sort of going together."

"Well, not exactly," I said. "To tell you the truth, I'm not sure what's going on between us." I shrugged. "Let's talk about something else. What's happening with Howorth Ranch?"

That led into a fifteen-minute conversation about a recent city council meeting in which they decided to appoint a committee to study future uses of the ranch. Apparently, my editorial (along with the petitions presented by the Save the Ranch people) had gone a long way towards convincing the council that further study needed to be done before any significant decisions were made.

Finally, I managed to work the conversation around to his family. "I wonder if you'd be into all this environmental stuff if you'd grown up in Indiana," I said.

"Who knows?" he replied. "My life would be a heck of a lot different, that's for sure."

Then he told me about his hometown, a little place called Feltonsburg. The countryside is beautiful, all rolling hills and woods and farmland, but the town itself is pretty dreary. Most of the shops went out of business back in the seventies when the biggest local industry (a steel mill) closed, and now downtown Feltonsburg is mostly boarded-up buildings. There's nothing to do—not even a video arcade or a movie theater—so most kids spend their weekends drinking beer and driving around in their pickup trucks, raising hell.

"Not many kids go to college," he said. "The girls get pregnant, the guys find some crummy job, and the cycle starts all over again."

"What about your birthmother?" I asked.

"She got pregnant with me just after graduation," he answered. "After the adoption, she got married—not to my birthfather. She divorced the guy last year. She works in a nursing home, delivering meals, changing bed pans, that kind of thing."

"And your birthfather?" I asked.

"Don't know. It was a one-night stand. All I know is that his name was Neil and he worked at a gas station. I have his eyes, Eileen says."

"When you met her—Eileen—what was it like?" I asked. "Did you feel sad? I mean, do you think you missed something by not spending time with your birthmother until now?"

Cody gazed out at the rolling waves, thinking. "Not really," he said at last. "It would have been weird trying to deal with two mothers when I was little. I don't know if I could have handled it."

"You couldn't have handled it?" I asked. "Or your parents wouldn't have let you?"

He smiled. "A little of both, I guess. My parents had a tough enough time dealing with my trip to Indiana. They would have freaked if Eileen had been hanging around when I was little."

"But maybe it would have worked," I insisted. "If your parents had been supportive, that is."

"Maybe. But I'm happy with the way things have turned out. I mean, I know Mom and Dad felt a little scared when I went to meet Eileen. Like what if I completely bonded with her and pushed them away or something? But it didn't work out that way."

According to Cody, in fact, it was just the opposite. Sure, he was glad he went to Indiana. The first time he looked at his birthmother, he said, it was like putting the last piece of a jigsaw puzzle into place. But being there with her didn't make him want to stay.

"In fact, it made me feel grateful to Eileen for choosing adoption," he said. He looked up and down the beach, as if he was seeing it for the first time. "Indiana's okay, but I've got an amazing life here. Besides, I wouldn't be on this beach right now, talking to you, if I hadn't been adopted. So as far as I'm concerned, things have worked out just fine."

I looked into Cody's eyes. He was gazing at me with intense concentration, as if he was trying to memorize every pore on my skin and every hair on my head. Suddenly, my face began to tingle and my cheeks grew hot. I could feel my heart throbbing inside my chest.

Cody jumped up and grabbed my hand. "Have you ever been surfing?" he asked.

"No," I stammered. "Wh—why?"

"Cuz you're going right now." He pulled me to my feet with so much force that I fell against him.

"Are you serious?" I laughed, staggering backward. "I don't even have a bathing suit with me. Besides, I've never been on a surfboard in my life."

"You can swim, can't you?" I nodded. "That's all you need to do," he said, grabbing his board. "I'll take care of the rest. Now, put on my wetsuit and let's go."

I must have been crazy, but there was something about the determined look in Cody's eyes that made me do what he told me. I wrapped his towel around me, stripped down to my underwear, and pulled his wetsuit on. It was much too big and I'm sure I looked ridiculous, but he didn't laugh. He just took my hand and led me into the ocean.

The water was the temperature of a root-beer float. But how could I complain when Cody was wearing nothing but a pair of baggy blue bathing trunks? At his urging, I knelt on the board. He got on behind me and together we began paddling out into the surf.

When the first incoming wave hit us, I threw myself down on the board and grabbed it in a death grip. I came up sputtering. "This is insane!" I shouted over the pounding surf. "A penguin would be cold out here!"

"Shut up and paddle!" he yelled. "We're going to catch this wave."

I glanced up and saw a monstrous wall of water—at

the time it seemed about twenty feet tall—surging toward us. I let out a scream, but Cody swung the board around and began paddling hard. Suddenly, the world seemed to drop out beneath us. I gasped, and then I felt his hands on my waist, lifting me to my feet. I looked down, my heart slamming against my ribcage. We were standing on the surfboard, sliding down a mountain of water. We were surfing!

"Oh my God, this is incredible!" I shrieked.

The next thing I knew, the board pitched left and I pitched right. I hit the water head first and was sucked into what felt like an enormous washing machine. For a second, I panicked. Which way was up? I couldn't breathe!

An instant later, I popped to the surface like a cork. I sucked in air and laughed for joy. I had surfed a wave and lived to tell about it. I looked around for Cody, eager to share my excitement. But where was he? I treaded water and scanned the surf. Oh Lord, what happened to him?

At that very moment, he shot up out of the water right behind me, his curly hair hanging wet on his forehead, sand in his eyelashes, a big grin on his face. And then he kissed me—a wet, salty, fish-flavored kiss that made my whole body tingle. Suddenly, I wasn't cold anymore. I was warm and happy and high as a kite on Cody Zeller.

December 19

I'm writing this in Iris's van, by the light of a Shell gasoline sign. We're parked in a gas station and Iris is in the bathroom. Since I last wrote, the world has turned upside down. My life in Laguna Verde is over. I've left it all behind—torched it and run away. The future lies before me now, wide and welcoming like the freeway. Am I scared? Of course I am, Mystery Baby. But together we're going to make it—Iris, me, and you, Little Em. From this day on, we're a family. From this moment on, we're free!

It all began this afternoon. I was lounging on the deck behind my house—excuse me, my parents' house—eating ice cream and celebrating the fact that I'd just finished my second and last midterm exam. My big English paper was sitting in the den next to the computer, ready to hand in tomorrow. After that, there was nothing to worry about except convincing my parents not to have a stroke when they found out

I'd invited Iris over for brunch on Christmas morning. I wasn't too worried, though. I knew she'd made them a present (a set of placemats and napkins she sewed herself), and I figured when they saw them, they'd be much too touched and pleased to throw her out.

Mom and Dad weren't home, and since I knew they'd be working at the restaurant that evening, I had a pleasant feeling of freedom. I took a bite of ice cream and fantasized about how thrilled Iris was going to be when I gave her my Christmas present (a big box of assorted beads for jewelry-making, and two yards of amazing Indonesian fabric I'd found in a secondhand store). Then the doorbell rang.

When I opened it, my stomach clenched like a fist. It was Iris, and she looked as if she'd been in a boxing match. Her cheek was bruised and swollen, there was a cut on her upper lip, and she had a black eye.

"What happened?" I cried, bustling her inside and leading her to the sofa. She seemed to collapse into it. I sat down beside her.

"Eddie and I had a fight," she said. She wasn't obviously crying—her face was expressionless, her voice was soft and flat—but there were tears streaming down her cheeks. "He wanted me to ask your parents for more money, but I said no."

"And he hit you?" I asked, not wanting to believe it.

She nodded. "He was supposed to be saving the money I gave him for his motorcycle shop, but he's been blowing it on booze and grass. Fat chance I'm going to get more for him."

"You've been giving him your money?" I asked, incredulous. "Iris, I thought we talked about that. The money is for you and the baby."

"Don't you think I know that?" she snapped. She glared at me, then suddenly her face fell and she began to sob openly. "I thought . . . I thought he loved me," she whispered.

"So did I," I said. I felt angry, betrayed. "Iris, why didn't you tell me what was going on?"

She shook her head, trying to understand. "I guess because I didn't know myself," she said at last. "I just thought guys were like that. I mean, he's not that different from my father. Besides, you acted like you thought he was so sexy, so cool. I wanted you to think I had the perfect boyfriend. You've got everything going for you. I just wanted one thing in my life to be as good as yours." Her voice cracked on the last word, and she broke down, sobbing uncontrollably.

I threw my arms around her and let her cry into my shoulder. I wasn't mad anymore. Just stunned to realize that Iris thought I had everything going for me. Me, the girl with no useful talents, no real boyfriend, and a pair of uptight parents who view their only child as an embarrassing disappointment.

"Iris," I said, "I wish you could see yourself through my eyes. You're strong, you're brave, you're independent. You've got artistic talent I can only dream of. On top of all that, you're about to bring a new life into the world. If that isn't having everything going for you, I don't know what is."

Iris smiled through her tears. "I left him, Sara. All I took were my jewelry-making tools, my sewing machine, and some clothes. I waited until he fell asleep, then I got into the van and drove away."

"You did the right thing," I told her. "We're going to

take care of you now. Do you want to put some ice on your eye?"

Iris shook her head. "I just want to lie down. I feel so tired, I can't think straight."

So I led her to my room and she stretched out on my bed. By the time I walked to the door, she was asleep. I went back to the living room and sat down. A second later, I was on my feet again. I was feeling agitated, apprehensive, excited. I had told Iris we were going to take care of her, and I meant it. As far as I was concerned, that meant letting her move in with us, at least until the baby was born. But would my parents go for it?

By the time I heard their car in the driveway, I had convinced myself they would. After all, they had assured me that they truly cared about Iris. They had to realize that letting her stay with us for the last month of her pregnancy was the best possible thing for both her and the baby. All it was going to take, I felt certain, was a little persuasion on my part.

But as usual, when I looked to my parents for their approval and support, they let me down.

It's midnight now and I'm sitting in the L.A. train station with Iris, trying not to fall asleep. I'm dead tired, but Iris says if you doze off the security guards come around and throw you out. To say that things aren't turning out the way I'd planned would be the understatement of the century. But anything would be better than going back home where I'm not wanted— was never wanted. Listen, Em . . .

My parents came home about an hour after Iris fell

asleep, around four o'clock. I met them at the door and told them what had happened.

"I knew that loser was abusing her," my father said. "She should have never let him move back in."

Mom and Dad walked into the living room and began talking together as if I wasn't even there. "Do you think we can recover any of the money Iris gave him?" Mom asked.

"I doubt it," Dad replied, "but I'll call the lawyer tomorrow and ask."

"We don't want to put too much pressure on Eddie," Mom said. "If we alienate him, he might not sign the relinquishment papers."

"I don't think we need to worry about that," Dad told her. "Even if he wanted the child—which I doubt—the courts aren't going to give the baby to a known batterer."

Mom nodded thoughtfully. "We'd better make sure Iris calls the police and reports him. We want to get this incident down in black and white."

I stood there at the entrance to the living room, absolutely dumbfounded. "What is wrong with you people?" I finally blurted out. "All you can think about is you, you, you. What about Iris? She's the one who got beat up—or have you forgotten that?"

"We haven't forgotten about Iris," Dad said. "When she wakes up, we'll take her to the doctor, then drive her to the police to file a complaint. Then we'll get a restraining order on Eddie so he can't come around her apartment anymore."

"I think we should also call the local shelter for battered women and see if we can get Iris some counseling," Mom said. "Considering Iris's history, I think there's a good chance she'll go back to Eddie if she doesn't get some help."

"Iris isn't going back to Eddie and she doesn't need counseling," I said firmly. "What she needs is a place to stay and someone who cares about her."

"Yes, that's a good idea," Mom said. "Maybe she could spend a few days with Kenya's birthmother, Megan. I'll ask Janie for her number."

"I was talking about us," I practically shouted. "Iris needs to stay someplace where she can rest and relax, someplace far away from Ellwood and Eddie. She needs to stay here."

"Absolutely not," my father said, flinging out his arm like he was tossing my idea out the window. "The answer is no."

"Why not?" I cried. "It makes perfect sense. We've got plenty of room. Anyway, you're always obsessing about Iris—is she eating right, is she drinking, is she taking drugs? If she stayed with us until the baby was born, you could keep an eye on her twenty-four hours a day."

"You want her to move in?" my mother asked, like it was the most absurd thing in the world. She frowned and shook her head. "I just wouldn't feel comfortable, Sara. For me, the birth of this baby will be a joyful thing. But for Iris, the joy is all mixed up with feelings of sadness and loss. If she were living here, I'd feel I had to walk on eggshells around her, wondering if my happiness was causing her sorrow. It's too much to deal with, for me *and* for Iris. She wouldn't be happy here."

"How do you know?" I demanded. "Have you asked

her?" I didn't wait for Mom's reply. "Well, I have. She wants to stay here. In fact, she practically begged me."

That wasn't exactly true, but I'm pretty sure it was what Iris was feeling. I saw the relieved expression on her face when I told her we were going to take care of her. She was looking to me for help, and I knew there was no way I was going let my parents stop me from giving it to her.

My father turned to me. "This has got to stop," he told me. "When we first met Iris, she was perfectly satisfied with who we are and what we have to offer her and the baby. But you've been putting ideas into her head, trying to make us look like the bad guys."

"All I'm doing is looking out for Iris and making sure you and your hotshot lawyer don't walk all over her," I insisted. "Besides, you don't need me to make you look bad. You're doing a terrific job all by yourself."

"Sara, please be reasonable," my mother said in her martyr voice. "There are no accepted rules of etiquette for dealing with open adoption. We're trying to make the best of a very complex, very unusual situation. Can't you at least make an effort to help us?"

"What's so difficult?" I cried, throwing up my hands in frustration. "If you would just treat Iris like a human being instead of your own personal babymaking machine, you wouldn't need any rules of etiquette. For once in your lives, can't you just forget the rules and listen your heart?"

My father took a step toward me, his eyes flashing. It was so unlike him. He looked furious, really out of control. "You want emotion, you want passion?" he bellowed. "Well, here it is! I'm sick of your accusations!

Do you hear me? You may be a child, but I'm through handling you with kid gloves. I've had it!"

"Marty, please. Calm down," my mother said, hurrying over and touching his arm.

But Dad was so out of control, he didn't even hear her. He stuck his finger in my face and shouted, "If you ask me, you're the one who isn't treating Iris like a human being. You don't know any more about her needs and desires than you do about the kitchen workers down at the restaurant. They're just a cause to you, a symbol. And now you've chosen Iris to be your own personal charity case. Well, I won't stand for it. You're going to destroy this adoption just to satisfy your own childish need to rebel against authority."

"You are so sick!" I cried. "You see everything I do as an attack on you. Well, this has nothing to do with causes or symbols. Iris is my friend. I'm going to help her, and if you cared half as much about her baby as you say you do, you would, too."

Dad grabbed my arm and pulled me close until his face was only inches from mine. I looked at him, but I didn't know him. He was a stranger, and I was scared. "Let me make this perfectly clear," he said in a quiet voice that was much more chilling than his shouting one. "We are adopting Iris's baby. We are not adopting Iris. We already have a troubled, pain-in-the-ass teenager, and we don't want another. We don't even want the one we've got!"

"Stop!" my mother shouted suddenly. "Please, stop!" My father dropped my arm and we both turned to her. She looked defeated, totally beaten. "This adoption is over," she said in a hoarse whisper. "Do you hear me? I don't want to go through with it."

Now it was my mother who was the stranger. I couldn't believe what I was hearing. "But, Mom—" I began.

She held up her hand, cutting me off. Tears welled up in her eyes and her shoulders jerked up and down in silent sobs. "I thought adopting a baby would bring this family together," she said, her voice cracking with emotion, "but instead, it's tearing it apart." She shook her hands in front of her as if she could make Iris, the baby—and especially me—disappear. "I'm going to tell Iris right now," she said. "It's over."

She walked toward the hallway and I started after her. That's when I saw Iris. She was standing at the entrance of the hallway, watching us. A sick, nauseated feeling washed over me. I wondered how long she'd been there, wondered what she'd heard.

"Iris," my mother breathed.

"It's all right," she said in a proud voice. "I'm leaving right now. And don't worry about the money you gave me. I'll pay it all back. Every penny." With that, she ran across the living room and out the front door.

I looked at Mom and Dad. They looked completely stunned, like cartoon characters who'd just been beaned with a frying pan. I almost wanted to laugh. Instead, I turned to them and said, "There, are you happy now? You got rid of Iris and now you're getting rid of me, all in one easy step. You can go back to living your self-absorbed little lives exactly the way you used to before I was born. Have a good time, folks, cuz I'm outta here."

As the last word left my lips, I spun around and ran out the door. I could hear my parents calling my name, but I kept running, down the driveway and out into the street where Iris's avocado-green van was just starting to pull away. "Iris, wait!" I yelled, pounding on the back. "Stop! Stop!"

She did. I ran to the passenger door, flung it open, and jumped inside. "Let's get out of here," I said. She hesitated, but I looked her in the eye and said firmly and clearly, "I mean it, Iris. Drive."

She stepped on the gas and we were gone.

December 19—Later

DEAR FUTURE???,

I can't call you Little Sib anymore, because I'm not going to be your sister. So what will I be? There's no word for it—not in our culture, anyway—but I hope I'll be like an aunt to you, only better. Maybe more like a second mother. Whatever. The point is, I'm going to be there for you, Little One, to love you, to help raise you, to watch you grow up. Me and Iris. Together.

We're still in the train station, trying to look as if we're waiting for a train. There's no point in leaving until morning, because we have nowhere to go—not in the dark, anyway. But tomorrow our new life will begin. Until then, here's the rest of the story . . .

After we left my parents, Iris and I drove a couple of minutes in silence. Then she said, "I don't know where I'm going."

"Me, either," I told her.

She turned to look at me. "What do you mean?

You're going home. I'll drop you off whenever you say the word."

I shook my head. "They don't want me any more than they want you. Why should I go back?"

"But you have to," Iris protested. "You're still a kid."

"I'm fifteen," I said. "I can take care of myself."

I sounded pretty bold, but inside I was scared. Was I really running away from home? It's not as if I'd made that decision—not consciously, anyway. My only thought had been to get away from my parents and be with Iris. I wanted her to know that just because my mother and father were rejecting her didn't mean I was, too. But beyond that, I hadn't made any plans.

Now, however, I realized I didn't want to go back. I mean, what was the point? My parents didn't want me around, that was for sure. My father's words were still playing inside my head like a broken cassette: *We already have a troubled, pain-in-the-ass teenager, and we don't want another. We don't even want the one we've got.* Besides, what did I have to look forward to if I stayed? A lifetime of hearing my parents tell me how I'd screwed up their adoption plans. A lifetime of knowing that they wanted a new baby, but they didn't want me.

"I'm not going home," I said. "I'm staying with you and the baby."

Iris didn't answer right away. I glanced over at her. She was staring out the front window, her hands clenched around the steering wheel. In the glow of the oncoming headlights, I could see her bruised cheek. It looked swollen and painful. Her skin was pasty and there were dark circles under her eyes. "Iris," I asked, "are you okay?"

"I feel kind of dizzy," she said. "I think maybe I need to eat something."

"We're not far from The Spot," I told her. "Let's sit down, have some food, and figure out what we're doing."

Iris nodded, and I showed her the way. We parked in back and walked in. The Spot was packed with the usual Thursday evening crowd—kids from the junior college and high school, some adults on their way to a movie, a couple of families, maybe a trucker or two. I thought back to the last time Iris and I had been there together. That was the day I first told her I was certain she would be able to visit the baby after it was born. Back then, I still believed my parents were capable of breaking out of their rigid little shells and acting with compassion and understanding. I knew better now.

We took a seat near the back and ordered—a big plate of fries for me, a cheeseburger for Iris. When the food came, Iris took a bite of her burger and stared off into space, her brow furrowed in thought. "I'll talk to Megan," she said at last. "Maybe she can help me find another family who wants to adopt."

That surprised me, and it hurt a little, too. "You'd give the baby to someone else?" I asked.

"What choice do I have? I can't support this kid any better than I could before. It's worse, really. I don't even have a job, and who's going to hire me looking like this?" She leaned back to show off her round belly. There was no hiding it now; she was huge.

I looked at her and thought of you inside there, Little One. You're not an embryo anymore. You're a baby, a new person just waiting to be born. I tried to imagine you belonging to some other family, some people I didn't even know. I pictured them holding you, feeding you, rocking you to sleep. It made my heart ache.

"Where are you going to stay tonight?" I asked.

"I don't know," she said. "I can't go back to my apartment. And most of my friends were really Eddie's, so I don't want to call them." She shrugged uncertainly. "Maybe I'll call Megan. If I can find her number."

But what about me? I wondered. Would Megan let me stay at her house, too? I considered my other possibilities. Lauren? Forest? But their parents would immediately know that something was up and call my folks. I shook my head. No way was I going to let Mom and Dad drag me back home.

That's when it hit me. I could call Marc. He hadn't always come through for me when I'd needed him, I knew that, but this was different. Marc was the kind of guy who understood about breaking away, taking a stand, going out on a limb for what you believe in. I felt certain he would let Iris and me stay at his house for the night, and I was pretty sure his parents wouldn't ask any questions. Then tomorrow . . . well, I'd deal with that when it came.

"I think I know a place where we can stay tonight," I told Iris. "Wait here."

I walked back to the pay phone, dropped in a quarter, and dialed Marc's number. His father answered and called him to the phone. "Hey, Sara," Marc said. "What's up?"

I gave him the condensed story, finishing up with the fight I'd had with my parents and how I'd followed Iris out the door. "I can't go back there," I told him.

"So I was wondering . . . can we stay at your place tonight?"

"Tonight?" he repeated. "Uh, I don't know, Sara. My grandparents are here and we're leaving on a ski trip right after school tomorrow. Things are kind of hectic."

My heart dropped. "Oh," I said, trying to hide my disappointment. "I understand."

"I think it's totally cool you stood up to your parents, though. Hey, listen," he said, his voice suddenly upbeat, "did I tell you we're going to stage our final protest in the cafeteria tomorrow? And check this out—I went to a butcher store and got some cow's blood. We're going to wear butcher's smocks and splatter it all over our—"

"Marc," I broke in, "I'm not coming to school tomorrow. Didn't you hear what I told you? I left home. I'm running away."

There was a long silence. "You mean forever?"

"Yeah. I guess so." Was that what I meant? "Yes," I said, as much to myself as to him.

"Jeez." He sounded stunned. "I mean . . . wow. Where are you going to live?"

"I don't know. I'll figure something out." I felt suddenly scared. Somehow, I had assumed Marc would be totally supportive. In fact, I think deep down I was fantasizing that he'd want to go with me. Instead he sounded almost shocked, like some uptight grown-up, and it was shaking my confidence. "Marc, listen, I'm kind of broke," I said. "Do you think I could borrow some money?"

"How much? I only have about fifty dollars, and I haven't even started buying Christmas presents yet."

That's when it finally sunk into my thick skull that

Marc doesn't give a damn about me. I guess on some level I'd known that for a long time, but I just hadn't wanted to admit it. But now there was no denying it. The only person Marc cares about is Marc.

Without another word, I hung up the phone and trudged back to the table. Iris looked up and I shook my head. She sighed. "I think you'd better go home now, Sara."

"No way. I told you, I'm staying with you and the baby."

"Don't be a fool," she said. "You've got a bed waiting for you, a family . . ."

The bed part sounded pretty good. But when I tried to picture myself walking back through my front door and facing my parents, seeing the disappointment in their eyes, hearing their recriminations, I knew I couldn't go through with it. "You're my family now," I told Iris. "You and the baby." I reached across the table and squeezed her hand. "I'm not going back home. I can't. Please, let me stay with you."

Iris twisted her leather bracelet. Then she looked at the one on my wrist, the one she'd made for me. "I can't make you go back. If you want to stay with me, I guess . . ."

At that moment, Cody walked through the back door. He was with two friends, two guys I knew slightly from school. "Oh my God," I gasped.

"What is it?" Iris asked, spinning around to follow my gaze.

Before I could answer, Cody spotted me and started over. My head was spinning. There was no time to tell Iris who he was, or that he didn't know anything about the adoption. There was no time to even think.

"All the best people come to The Spot," Cody said, grinning as he stepped up to our table.

"Hi, Cody," I said. "This is my friend, Iris."

"Hi," he replied, his eyes drawn to her bulging stomach. He smiled. "When's your baby due?"

"Next month," she told him. She turned to me. "This is the guy you told me about, right?"

Cody laughed. "Only the good stuff, I hope."

I smiled nervously and nodded. "Yeah, he's the one."

Iris gave me a look that clearly said, "Aren't you going to tell him what's going on?"

I didn't say anything. What could I say? Part of me was dying to tell Cody what had happened. I mean, if anyone would understand, it was him. But the thought of blurting it all out now, when I'd kept the adoption a secret for so long, was just too weird.

I gazed up into his clear blue eyes. They looked so kind, so sympathetic. Unlike Marc, Cody didn't think the whole world revolved around him. I began to think maybe I could tell him. I even imagined he might be able to help us.

"Cody, there's something I haven't told you," I began in a shaky voice. "My family was planning to adopt Iris's baby. But tonight my parents broke their promise to Iris and told her they don't want the baby. So Iris and I left, and we're not going back."

Cody looked completely bewildered. "Your family is trying to adopt?" he said at last. "But why didn't you tell me, Sara?"

I shrugged, flustered and embarrassed. "I don't know. I guess I didn't want you to think the only reason I was talking to you was because Lauren told me you were adopted."

"Lauren told you that?" he asked. I nodded. "And that's why you came up to me that day outside the cafeteria?" he continued. "So you could pick my brain about adoption?"

"Yes, at first," I admitted.

"Now I know why you kept asking me about my family," he said. "I thought it was kind of odd the way you wanted to hear every detail." He laughed softly. "I convinced myself it was because you were so fascinated with me."

"But I was," I said. "I mean, I am. Cody, listen. After I got to know you, I started to like you for yourself. I started to—"

I was going to say "really care about you," but I never finished the sentence because Cody cut me off.

"I'm not a specimen in a laboratory—some kind of representative adopted person you can examine and label," he said. "I'm me, an individual."

"I know you are," I told him. "And I meant to tell you about Iris and everything, really I did. It's just—"

"It's just that you thought you couldn't get me to really open up if I knew the truth." He smiled sadly. "I really liked you, Sara. But it looks like you were more interested in what you could get out of me than in really getting to know me. That hurts."

I shook my head. "It wasn't like that. Cody, please." I reached out and touched his arm. "Sit down and let's talk."

"No, thanks. My friends are waiting for me." He pulled his arm away and thrust his hand into his pocket. "I'll see you around, Sara."

Tears were welling up in my eyes and I clamped my throat shut, trying to stop them. I just couldn't believe Cody was going to walk away—not now, when I needed him so much. "Didn't you hear what I just told you?" I pleaded. "My parents threw Iris out of the house and I left with her. We're not going back. We're going to raise the baby ourselves."

Cody stopped and stared at me in disbelief. Out of the corner of my eye, I could see Iris staring at me, too. I don't know why I'd said we were going to raise the baby ourselves. But the minute the words left my lips, I knew it was the only possible option.

"Don't be an idiot," Cody said. "Two teenage girls can't raise a baby right. Where are you going to live? What are you going to do for money?"

Cody's words stung. I'd expected support from him— sympathy, at the very least—but he was acting as if the whole thing was an absurd joke. "We'll work it out," I said defensively. "We can find jobs. I don't know, maybe borrow some money . . ."

"Oh, that's a brilliant idea." He pulled a couple of dollar bills out of his pocket. "Let's see. I must have all of five or six dollars. You'll get real far on that."

"Listen to you," I cried, my defensiveness turning to rage. "Just because you were adopted doesn't mean every unplanned pregnancy has to end that way. We can give this baby as good a home as my parents could have. Better, because we really want her."

Cody tossed the dollars on the table. "I can't stop you. Do what you want. You aren't going to listen to me anyway."

"Hang on," I said, suddenly wary. "You're not going to call my parents, are you?"

Cody shook his head. "Don't worry, I'm not going to

tell anyone I saw you." He let out a sigh. "So long, Sara. I just hope you know what you're doing."

"I do," I said, and I meant it. There's no way I'm going to let someone else raise you, Mystery Baby. You belong to Iris and me. But first I had to make Iris realize it, too.

Cody walked away and I turned to her. Suddenly, Cody's rejection of me didn't seem to matter. My head was buzzing with ideas and plans. Everything was falling into place. It all made sense. "Let's do it," I told her.

Iris looked disbelieving, but hopeful. "But how?" she asked. "Where?"

"In L.A.," I said. "We'll drive down and sell your jewelry and handmade clothes to the trendy shops on Melrose Avenue. Once we get some orders, we can rent an apartment. I'm sure I can get some kind of job, too. When the baby comes, we'll take turns taking care of her. Then someday, after we've saved up enough money, you can open your own shop, just the way we talked about."

Iris smiled. "It's a nice dream. I'd like to believe it."

"It's not a dream," I insisted. "We're going to do it. We don't need boyfriends or parents or adoptive couples who want to take your baby and dump you. We can make it on our own."

Iris looked at me. I knew she was just as scared and excited as I was.

"We'll drive to L.A. tonight and sleep in the van," I said. "Then tomorrow we can show your stuff to the shop owners on Melrose."

Iris was still silently watching me.

"Say yes," I told her. "Say you'll drive to L.A. with me right now."

I stretched my hand across the table, palm up. Iris hesitated, then took my hand and squeezed it hard. She nodded her head and smiled a small, closed-mouth smile. "Okay," she said, "let's go."

December 19—Later Still

It was almost seven o'clock when we left Laguna Verde. In the back of the van, Iris had some extra clothes, her handmade vests and jewelry, her sewing machine, a few toiletries. I had nothing except the clothes on my back and the contents of my fanny pack—five dollars and fourteen cents. Even so, I felt good. I was scared, yes. But it was a good scared, an exhilarated scared, like when you get to the top of a roller coaster and find yourself staring into nothingness.

Nothingness. I have plenty of that, all right. I keep thinking about Cody and the disgusted look on his face when he threw down the dollar bills and said, "Do what you want. You aren't going to listen to me anyway." I mean, Marc's rejection hurt, but Cody's was like being hit by a truck. That's because little by little, I'd been falling in love with him. I hadn't admitted it to myself, but I know now it's true.

Only now it's over. Cody thinks I used him, and I suppose I did. But didn't he use me, too, when he asked me to go hiking with him, and then talked me into helping him with his Save the Ranch letter? Anyway, so what if I used him a little bit, just at the beginning? I apologized, didn't I? And I told him I really like him. What more does he want?

Forget it. I'll probably never see Cody again, so I might as well get used to it. That's what I told Iris, and she knew how I felt because she's never going to see Eddie again, either. And even though he treated her bad, I guess she loved him, too.

Sorry, Mystery Baby, I'm getting off the subject. I suppose it's because I'm wet and cold and so exhausted I can barely think straight. Anyway, where was I?

Iris and I were driving down the freeway, singing along with the radio and making plans for the future. I opened the window so we could hear the waves splashing against the concrete barriers at the side of the road. It reminded me of the last time we went to L.A. together, when we were riding on the train and saw the dolphins splashing in the waves. If anyone had told me then that Iris and I would soon be running away to L.A. to raise her baby, I never would have believed it. But there we were, driving through the darkness, singing along to that stupid oldie that goes, "it never rains in California . . ."

Yeah, right. A couple of minutes later, it started to pour. That's when Iris found out that the van's windshield wipers work in slow motion—or at least, that's the way it seemed. Anyway, what with the rain and the fogged-up windows (the defroster doesn't work too well, either), we could barely see the white lines on the road.

So we stopped at the Shell station. We figured we'd sit in the van until the rain slowed up. Only when it did—two hours later—the stupid van wouldn't start. The engine wouldn't even turn over. Luckily, there was a mechanic on duty at the gas station. But when he looked under the hood, he came up shaking his head. The starter motor had burned out, the carburetor was filled with gunk, and the battery was dead. Altogether, he estimated it would cost at least two hundred bucks to get the thing running again.

"How much money do you have?" I asked Iris.

"Around sixty dollars," she answered.

I was shocked. I'd figured she had a couple hundred, at least. "What happened to all the money my parents gave you?"

"I told you," she said. "I gave it to Eddie."

"Terrific. What are we going to do now?"

"Hitchhike, I guess," she said. "Either that or go back."

I shook my head. "We're not going back. No way."

So we talked to the mechanic and convinced him to let us leave the van at the gas station for two weeks. If we didn't come back to claim it by then, it was his. I figured in two weeks we'd easily have enough money to pay for the repairs. Anyway, what choice did we have?

We grabbed the two duffel bags containing Iris's stuff and headed up the road to the freeway entrance. The rain had slowed to a steady drizzle. Still, it didn't take long to turn our clothes damp and clammy.

"Have you ever done this before?" I asked, watching the cars whiz past us onto the freeway.

"Hitchhike? It's easy," Iris said. "Just stick out your thumb and smile."

She was right. Within two minutes, we were picked up by a middle-aged Latino guy in a pickup truck. We tossed the duffel bags in the back. I got in first and Iris sat by the window.

"What are you girls doing out on a night like this?" he asked. He had to reach between my legs to move the stick shift. I quickly threw both legs on the right side of the stick and leaned against Iris.

"Going to L.A.," she said. "How about you?"

He didn't answer. "Didn't anyone ever tell you thumbing rides is dangerous? You can get picked up by all kinds of crazies."

Like you? I wondered, but my fears turned out to be groundless. Without another word, he flipped on the radio and turned up the volume. We spent the next thirty minutes listening to mariachi music. Finally, he took an exit in Studio City and let us out at the light.

"Vaya con Dios," he said before he drove away. "And call your parents, okay, girls?"

We nodded and headed across the street to the freeway entrance. "The fatherly type," Iris said. "The best kind of ride you can get—unless he drives you to the police station and turns you in."

"What's the worst?" I asked.

"A serial killer, I guess," she said with a dark laugh. Then she stopped smiling. "Drunks are bad. And cokeheads. And horny guys who think a girl with her thumb out is fair game."

I stood in the rain, shivering and fondly remembering Iris's van. So what if it had wire springs sticking through the seat cushions and the suspension system of a tank? At least it was warm and dry.

"Where are we going to sleep tonight?" I asked Iris.

"We aren't," she said. "But if we make it to a train station or a bus terminal, at least we can dry off and wait for morning."

"How about Union Station?" I suggested. "It's got benches and everything."

It only took one more ride to get us to L.A. Unfortunately, it was with a carload of rowdy twenty-something slackers who were heading to a party in Whittier. Iris and I had to squeeze in the back with two of them. There were two more in the front. We'd barely hit the freeway when they pulled out a joint and started passing it around. The tape deck was blasting seventies disco music.

"You girls like to party?" the boy beside me shouted. He was a big guy with greasy blond hair and chapped lips.

"We're going to a rave," the driver yelled. "You wanna come with us?"

"Sure they do," the dark-haired guy in the passenger seat said. "What are they doing out here hitchhiking if they aren't looking for a good time?"

"We're going to Los Angeles," I said. "On business. Our car broke down. We've got a business meeting in the morning."

"You're stranded, huh?" the boy beside me asked with a grin. "I've got a place you can stay."

I felt something slide across my leg. I looked down. It was his hand.

Iris saw it, too. "Get your hand off her," she said.

The boy on her other side, chunky with a shaved head, put his arm around her. "Don't worry about your friend," he said with an evil grin. "Worry about me."

Iris opened her jacket to reveal her swollen stomach. "Lay off," she said. "I'm pregnant."

"So what?" he cracked. "As long as you're not dead, you're all right with me."

His buddies burst out laughing. Iris reached in her jacket pocket. There was a flash of metal. I leaned forward in the darkness, straining to see. My mouth fell open when I realized Iris was holding a knife.

"Let us out at the next exit or I'll slit your throat," she said, pointing the knife at the chunky guy's Adam's apple.

The greasy guy took his hand off my leg so fast you would have thought it was on fire.

"Christ!" the chunky guy cried. "Let 'em out, Del. They're wackos."

The driver glanced in the rearview mirror. His mouth dropped open. He hit the gas hard and we tore down the freeway toward the next exit. I was staring at Iris, my eyes bugging out of my head. I had no idea she carried a knife—or that she had the guts to use it.

"Here you go," Del said in a shaky voice, pulling off the Sixth Street exit in downtown L.A. "Now put that thing away before you hurt someone."

Iris threw open the door and climbed out. I followed, my knees shaking. The slackers roared away, their tires squealing.

"Oh, my God!" I gasped. "Where did you get that knife?"

"It's my brother's. I took it with me when I left home." She flipped the switchblade shut and put it back in her pocket. "It's gotten me out of some tight situations."

I don't know why, but I started to giggle. Iris joined in, and pretty soon we were both laughing so hard we could barely catch our breath. It's so weird to think of us standing there at the side of the freeway exit, the rain (no drizzle now) pouring down on us, just laughing ourselves silly. Anyone watching us would have thought we were lunatics. But at that moment, it felt absolutely right.

Finally, we just couldn't laugh anymore. I looked at Iris. Her auburn hair was hanging in wet tendrils on her forehead. "How far to Union Station?" she asked.

"You don't want to know." I turned up my collar and grabbed a duffel bag. "Start walking."

So that's how we ended up here, sitting in Union Station, trying to look like we're waiting for a train. I've never felt so damp or exhausted or hungry (no dinner, remember? Just that plate of fries at The Spot) in my entire life.

But tomorrow will be different. Tomorrow we'll hit Melrose, line up some craft orders for Iris, and find an apartment. Tomorrow night, Mystery Baby, you'll be well-fed, out of the rain, sleeping on a bed. That's a promise, from your Mommy and me.

December 20

Okay, Mystery Baby, I know things didn't turn out exactly the way I planned. But I kept my promise, didn't I? You're out of the rain, well-fed (if you can call the chili dog Iris ate for dinner food), and Iris is sleeping on a bed (well, a mattress, anyway). As for me, I'm writing this by the glow of the streetlight outside our window. The wail of police sirens mix with the sounds of broken glass, thumping bass lines, and car horns. Don't people ever go to bed in this neighborhood? I'd sure like to. Instead, I'm gazing at the stars above the apartment buildings, dreaming of a better tomorrow. For me, for Iris, and especially for you.

When morning came, the rain stopped. We washed our faces and brushed our hair in the restroom (Iris let me use her brush), then left Union Station and bought ourselves some breakfast. I was in favor of splurging on eggs and pancakes—after all, I was sure we'd have more money by evening, and besides, my stomach was growling like an angry dog. But Iris insisted we save our cash (all sixty-six dollars and fourteen cents of it), just in case. With that thought in mind, she bought a raisin bagel and some coffee. I opted for an onion bagel and orange juice. My throat hurt and I was hoping the Vitamin C would help.

Then we took the bus—a couple of buses, actually—over to Melrose Avenue. The shops were still closed when we got there, so we wandered up and down the street, window-shopping. What bizarre, amazing, hyper-hip stuff those shops sell—everything from chattering teeth to $300 shoes; Mexican "Day of the Dead" art to 1956 Coke machines; and secondhand clothing once worn by famous people to gorgeous handmade furniture.

Iris was stunned. "People actually buy this stuff?" she asked. I nodded. "But that old Coke machine costs a thousand bucks!" she exclaimed, pointing at the sign in the window.

"Hey, this is L.A.," I said. "People have more money than they know what to do with."

"Not all of them," she replied, tilting her head to indicate a homeless woman who was coming toward us, pushing a shopping cart full of junk. Every few seconds, she stopped and shouted something unintelligible at the sky.

Iris reached into her duffel bag. As the woman passed, she handed her a dollar bill. The woman smiled and said, "God bless you," then shouted her gibberish to the clouds and moved on.

"Why did you do that?" I asked, irritated. "You wouldn't even let me buy a decent breakfast."

"Because I felt sorry for her," she answered. "And because I might be in her shoes someday."

"No way. Not after you start selling your hand-made clothing."

Iris turned to me and smiled sheepishly. "When we go into the stores, you do the talking, okay?"

I rolled my eyes. What was so tough about asking people to look at the stuff you made? Especially if it was either that or starve to death. "Why don't you take out your finished work so I can see what we're trying to sell," I said, avoiding her question.

We stopped at a bus stop and laid the duffel bags on the bench. She pulled out two wrinkled vests and three pairs of earrings.

"That's it?" I asked. "I figured you'd made more by now."

Iris shrugged. "It was easy to make things when they were just for me, but how should I know what other people want?"

"What's the big deal?" I asked. I was getting really frustrated. "Just make what you like and other people will want it. Like the bracelet you made me. The minute I saw yours, I wanted one."

"Okay, okay," she said. "Don't get mad."

I frowned. "This isn't enough stuff to show the store owners. Pull out some of the clothing you made for yourself—like that blouse you were wearing the first time I met you."

"But I love that one," she protested. "Besides, it was Eddie's favorite."

"Who cares what Eddie likes," I snapped. "He's not here to help you now."

Iris's cheeks blazed red, and she turned away. I

wished I'd kept my mouth shut, but before I could apologize, the neon sign above a nearby store flashed on. It was the name of the store, WISECRACKERS, in blue and yellow with a red firecracker underneath. A sales clerk unlocked the door and pushed it open. I looked in the window. The place sold everything from clothing to writing paper to incense.

"Come on," I said. "Let's get started. And think positive. Remember, you are an artist." I gazed at Iris's glum face. "And smile," I urged.

Iris picked up her vests and her jewelry, I grabbed the duffel bags, and we walked inside. "Can we talk to the owner?" I asked the sales clerk, a skinny girl with pale skin and a henna-red crew cut.

"She isn't in today."

"How about the manager? We have some incredible handmade clothing and jewelry to show her—or him. I know it would sell really well in here."

"We're not buying now," the girl said in a bored voice. "Try back in a couple of months."

"But—" I began.

"I said we're not buying. Now unless you're a customer, I'm going to have to ask you to leave."

I shot the clerk a disgusted look and we trudged out into the street. Iris gazed at me with a "I knew that wouldn't work" expression. "Come on," I said, wondering why it was always me who had to give the pep talks. "That was only the first store. There are dozens of others."

But up and down the street, it was all the same. Either the owner/manager/buyer wasn't in, or they weren't buying, or they bought all their merchandise through distributors. A couple of shops said they'd get back to us and asked for our business card, which of course we didn't have, or our phone number, which we didn't have either.

"What's the matter with these people?" I said as we walked out of a store called Muse. "Are they all too bored and stupid to recognize something beautiful when they see it?"

Iris shrugged. "We're nobodies. They probably want crafts made by people they've heard of already."

But I refused to give up. My perseverance paid off, too, when after two hours of rejection, we came to a shop called Strange But True. It was filled with antique costume jewelry, old sepia photographs, and dusty books, and at first I figured, why even bother? But we went in anyway, and much to our surprise, the sales-clerk said she liked Iris's stuff. She wasn't the owner, she said, but she'd been authorized by the owner to acquire anything that caught her eye. The only catch was, she could only take Iris's stuff on consignment—in other words, we don't get any money up front. But if (when) it sells, Iris earns forty percent.

Well, what choice did we have? I mean, it was better than nothing. Besides, we liked Jade, the salesclerk. She was friendly—something most of the bored, I'm-so-hip clerks in the other stores hadn't been—and she seemed really enthusiastic about Iris's stuff. So we said yes. We're supposed to check back in a week to see if anything has sold. Meanwhile, Jade wants Iris to start work on more jewelry and some clothing. (Ha—her favorite item was the blouse Iris hadn't wanted to sell. See, Iris, I told you so.)

By the time we'd tried all the stores on the hip part of Melrose (about a mile up one side and a mile back on the other), I was beat. I looked at Iris. Her face was the same pale, pasty color it had been the first time I met her—the time she'd almost fainted. "How are you doing?" I asked.

"Not great. I need to eat something."

So we went to Johnny Rockets and ordered some lunch—a burger for Iris, and a grilled-cheese sandwich for me. It set us back seven dollars and fifty-three cents. While we ate, we made plans.

"Okay," I said, "so we find a place to live, and you start making some more jewelry and clothing. Meanwhile, I'll go out and look for a job."

But Iris said we couldn't rent an apartment with fifty-five dollars, because the landlord would expect us to pay first and last month's rent, plus a security deposit. She said we could buy a paper and try to find a room in a shared apartment, or get a room in a building that rents by the week. I voted for the second option; I mean, I didn't leave home just so I could live with a bunch of strangers. Besides, Iris said that a by-the-week place would be cheaper.

We finished our food and went outside. We had no idea where to find rooms for rent, so we asked a couple of people on the street. A young punk with a nose ring and a pierced lip told us to head over to Edgemont Street and Beverly Boulevard.

It was a long walk and by the time we got there, Iris's ankles were swollen. I sat her down on a doorstep with our duffel bags, and went to look for a place. The neighborhood was pretty scary—boarded-up buildings, garbage in the gutter, a couple of nasty-looking dudes exchanging money in an alleyway. I reminded myself that soon we'd be moving to a real apartment. Then I went into the first place I saw that advertised rooms for rent.

It was called the Edgemont Arms. The lobby had a dirty tile floor and institutional green walls. The desk clerk, a middle-aged guy with a stomach that hung over his belt, was sitting in a booth, like a guy selling tickets at a movie theater. He said the cheapest room was thirty-five dollars a week, so I took it. It only had a single bed, but I figured we could put the mattress on the floor for Iris, and I'd sleep on the box springs. I pushed the money through the window and he gave me a key.

I went back to get Iris, and we climbed the stairs to our room. It was on the fifth floor, in the middle of a long hallway. The bathroom was at the end of the hall, a tiny room with a dirty sink, a toilet, and a tub with lime deposits around the drain. Our room was about the size of my bedroom at home. It had two windows, a stained orange rug on the floor, a metal bed, a metal bureau, and two metal straight-backed chairs.

"What a hole!" I groaned.

"I've seen worse," Iris said. She sat down on the bed and took off her shoes.

"Lie down," I said. "I'm going to go look for a job."

"Don't tell them your real age," she advised. "Say you're eighteen."

Which I did, but I still struck out. Most of the businesses I tried weren't hiring, and the only one that was—a hot-dog stand called the Dog House—didn't believe I was eighteen and asked for I.D. Finally, after combing ten square blocks, I went back home—or what passes for home right now. My feet were aching and my head was pounding. Iris wasn't doing much better.

She had slept most of the time I was gone, and she said she felt groggy and weak.

When I told her about my job hunt, she rubbed her face with her hands. "I knew it," she said. "Why did I listen to you? We're crazy if we think we can raise this kid alone. We can't even feed ourselves, let alone a baby."

"Why are you so negative all the time?" I asked angrily. "I can find a job. I just have to look harder. And you already have one. Tomorrow you can start making some more clothes and jewelry for Strange But True."

"Tomorrow I'll be working at that hot dog stand, if they'll hire me," she said. "What did you say it was called? The Dog House?"

I didn't answer. Iris stared at me a second, then put on her shoes, grabbed her jacket, and walked out the door.

I let her go. I was too mad to care, and besides, I figured she'd never find the Dog House. I flopped down on the bed and stared at the cracks in the ceiling. I couldn't understand why Iris was acting as if everything that had happened was my fault. I mean, she was the one who handed over all her money to Eddie. If we had that cash now, we'd be sitting in a real apartment instead of this crappy dump.

Besides, what had happened that was so horrible? Iris's handmade clothing and jewelry were on the shelves of a hip Melrose Avenue store. We had a roof over our heads, even if it was kind of cracked and sagging. And most of all, we were together. The way I saw it, if it weren't for me, Iris would be back in Ellwood, broke and alone, desperately searching for someone—anyone—to adopt her baby. She'd probably even wind up crawling back to Eddie.

With those thoughts in my head, I dozed off. When I woke up, it was getting dark. I sat up with a gasp, wondering where I was. Then I figured it out and jumped up to turn on the light. I was alone. Where was Iris?

I went outside and roamed the streets, searching for her. What if someone had mugged her, or even worse? And then another thought struck me. Maybe she had left me and gone back to Ellwood, or even taken off down the road for points unknown. I felt a horrible wave of anxiety wash over me. I didn't want to be here without Iris, and I sure as hell didn't want to go home. Besides, after everything that had happened, my parents probably wouldn't even let me.

I was heading back to the Edgemont Arms, my stomach churning with fear and dread, when I saw Iris walking down the sidewalk toward me. I ran to meet her, my heart pounding. "Where were you?" I cried. "I was scared to death."

"The Dog House hired me," she said with a smile. "They wanted me to start work right away. I get my first paycheck next week. Not only that, I brought food."

I let out a whoop of joy. How could I be mad when we had food? But when we got back to the room I found out the bag she was carrying contained nothing but hot dogs. "I can't eat this," I said. "It's meat."

"It's food," she answered. "Anyway, this is all they would let me take."

"Let's go to a restaurant," I begged. "We still have money."

"We won't if we keep eating out," Iris said. She thrust a hot dog in my face. "Now go on, eat."

I ate the rolls, but I was still starving. Finally, I gagged down a few bites of hot dog. God, it was gross. I thought about you, Mystery Babe, and tried to imagine what our lives will be like when you're old enough to start eating solid food. I don't want you to be forced to eat junk just because we don't have the money to give you something better. Because money means options, Kiddo, and right now that's something we don't have.

So here we are. Iris was exhausted, so we pulled the mattress onto the floor and she went to bed. I tried to sleep on the box springs, but they're awfully bumpy and hard. Besides, I'm too wired to sleep. Outside, a police helicopter is shining its searchlights up and down the street. The noise is enough to wake a dead man.

Or an unborn baby. According to that birth book I got out of the library, Mystery Baby, you can hear sounds from the outside world. Loud noises make your heart beat faster and your entire body tremble. Are you trembling now, Little One? Me, too. But hang in there. I'm looking beyond the glare of the helicopter's lights, up to the stars, and I'm making a wish just for you.

December 23

DEAR BABY,

I hope you won't be mad at me when you grow up and read this. Things aren't going so great for you right now—or for your mother and me, either.

Iris has been working nine-hour shifts at the Dog House. She doesn't get paid until next week, though, so money's kind of tight. We bought some bread and peanut butter, and we've been living on that. Iris also eats any hot dogs that are left over at the end of her shift. She always brings home one for me, but just looking at it makes me want to barf. Still, I force myself to eat a few bites if I have a pounding headache— something I've been having a lot lately. For some weird reason, artificially flavored, nitrate-ridden chili dogs seem to help.

When Iris isn't at the Dog House she's in our room, sewing or making jewelry. Only problem is, she's been at it for three days now and she's only finished one vest and two pairs of earrings. She seems to work in slow motion, and she's getting slower every day. A couple of times I even caught her hunched over her sewing machine, fast asleep. Then it's up to me to wake her up. She always acts totally disoriented, just really out of it. One time she actually smiled up at me and said, "Hey, Eddie, how about a kiss?"

God, I feel like such a creep making her work so hard. I know she's exhausted, and she comes home from the Dog House every day with her ankles swollen and her back aching. But what can I do? I've been pounding the pavement, but I still haven't been able to find a job—except yesterday when I talked a woman into paying me two dollars to clean up all the garbage that had fallen out of her trash cans after some animal had knocked them over. Yech, what a disgusting job. There was rotten fish and dirty diapers everywhere.

I asked Iris to teach me how to sew and make jewelry, and she's been trying. When she's at work, I practice sewing hems and bending wire with her needle-nose pliers. But it's going to take a while before I'm good enough to actually help her make anything.

To complicate our lives even further, we've had to change apartment buildings every day. That's because Wednesday morning, after we went out to buy the bread and peanut butter, we came home to find two cops in the lobby of the Edgemont Arms. They were questioning the guy in the little booth and he was shaking his head no, no, no.

There was no way to tell for sure, but Iris said the cops might be looking for us. So we hightailed it down the alley and waited until they left. Then we checked out and moved into another building a couple of miles away with rooms to rent. Just to be on the safe side, we're going to change apartment buildings every day, at least for a while.

You should see the slum we're living in now. Well, actually, Mystery Baby, I'd rather you didn't. I mean, the wall of our room looks like it has blood smeared across it. I try not to think where it came from. The guy next door sounds like he's coming off drugs. We can hear him through the walls, sobbing and shouting for someone named Vince. The only good thing about this place is that it's cheap—only six bucks a night.

Being on my own is different from the way I thought it would be. Sure, I got what I wanted—no parents around telling me what to do, and lots of free time— but without school or a job to go to, the days get kind of long. I mean, there's not a heck of a lot to do. No television, no cassette tapes or CDs, not even a magazine to read. We've only been gone four days, but I already miss my room, my soft bed, my books. I even miss those stupid veggie burgers.

During the day, when Iris is at work and I'm not job-hunting or practicing my sewing, I wander the streets, just checking out the people. L.A. is quite a scene, Mystery Baby. There are movie execs driving Range Rovers, deal-making on their car phones; Mexican gardeners with their dueling leaf blowers, blasting dust and litter back and forth from one yard to another; Orthodox Jewish moms with scarves over their heads, joking in Yiddish as they walk their kids to school; heavy metal boys with poodle haircuts and Flying V guitars; and punks with tattoos and pierced eyebrows.

Sometimes it scares me to think of raising you here, Little One. I'd always dreamed of leaving dead end Laguna Verde and moving to L.A., but that was before

I took on the responsibility of a baby-to-be. Now some little town in Iowa is starting to sound appealing. At least there you can sleep through the night without a police helicopter shining its lights in your window.

It's so weird to think that Christmas is only two days away. All the stores are decorated with twinkling lights and mistletoe, and there are Salvation Army guys outside every department store, singing carols and ringing their bells. Back home, my parents have probably bought a tree by now. We always wait until Christmas Eve to decorate it. I wanted to buy a tree for Iris and me, just a little one, but she said no way. We can't waste the money. So I stole some pine branches off a gas station wreath and stuck them around the window. At least they make the place look a little bit more festive.

Last night I dreamed about our Christmas tree. When I was little, Dad used to lift me up to put the star on the top. He still tries, then laughs and says, "Let's get the ladder." It's become a private joke between us. Anytime he sees me reaching up to get something out of a kitchen cabinet, he grabs me around the waist and lifts me, then pretends he's thrown out his back. Then I say, "Let's get the ladder." Dumb, I know, but it always makes us laugh.

Only I guess Dad won't be saying that this year. Sometimes I find myself wondering what he and Mom have been doing since I left. Are they worried out of their minds, lying awake at night, questioning my friends about where I am, hiring private detectives to find me, bursting into tears every time they hear my name? Or are they looking forward to spending Christmas alone, their first since I was born?

The more I think about it, the more I'm convinced

those cops in the lobby of the Edgemont Arms weren't looking for Iris and me. I don't think my parents are trying to find me; or even want to. I think Iris and I are in exactly the same boat. Our parents are happy we're out of their hair.

Oh, Mystery Baby, sometimes I feel so scared. I'm completely alone in the world now, except for Iris and you. And Iris and I seem to be growing more and more distant every day. I mean, we almost never laugh together anymore or talk about the future. And of course, there's no reason to talk about boyfriends or my parents. Sometimes it seems all we do is argue about money. Iris is so rigid about things. She won't let me buy a hot plate so we can start cooking vegetarian food in our room. She wouldn't let me buy a Christmas tree. She won't even let me buy underwear. I mean, can you believe it? She makes me wash out my one lousy pair of underpants every night and wear them again the next day.

It's almost starting to feel as if Iris is my big sister instead of my friend. Okay, so maybe she *is* three years older than me. And maybe she's spent a lot more time living on her own than I have. Big deal. I'm not a baby. If it weren't for me, she'd still be under my parents' thumb, and she certainly wouldn't be selling her clothes and jewelry on Melrose Avenue.

Anyway, what I'm trying to say is, I can't wait to meet you, Mystery Baby. Unlike the rest of the world, you're going to really, truly love me. I keep imagining what it will feel like to cradle you in my arms and gaze into your eyes. We're going to be best friends, Little One. You and me.

*   *   *

I had to stop writing because Iris came home from work early. She fainted while she was taking somebody's order and hit her head on the counter when she fell. The other workers wanted to call an ambulance, but Iris refused. Then she got up and went back to work. But then the owner showed up, and when he heard what had happened, he told Iris he couldn't be responsible for the physical safety of a woman who is eight months pregnant and obviously not in good health. Then he fired her.

Damn. Everything is so screwed up. I just feel like screaming, only there's no one to hear me except Iris and she's trying to sleep, so why bother? The only good part of what happened is that Iris got paid (in cash, no less), so now we have one hundred and thirty-five dollars. Of course, as my annoying big sister Iris pointed out, we can't spend it except on necessities, because we don't know when we'll have any more coming in.

I've decided to prove her wrong by taking the new vest and earrings she made over to Strange But True. Or am I just trying to convince myself? I don't know, but I've got a hunch the stuff we left there on Tuesday has sold. After all, it's gift season and Jade seemed to think that Iris's crafts will practically leap off the shelf.

Man, won't Iris be blown away if I come home with a handful of money and an order for more vests and blouses and jewelry? Who knows? She might even let me buy a Christmas tree.

Wish me luck, Mystery Baby. Here goes nothing.

December 24

Everything is screwed up. I don't even know where to begin. But I've got to get it all down on paper. Mystery Baby, this journal isn't for you anymore. It's for me. I've got to write down what's happening so maybe I can make some kind of sense of it. And I've got to keep myself busy, force myself to move the pen across the paper so I won't break down and start to cry.

I went back to Strange But True. Iris's stuff wasn't on the shelves, so of course I assumed it had sold. Man, I was walking on air. I couldn't wait to get the money and take it to Iris. So I went up to the counter and asked for Jade. A tall black guy wearing gold earrings told me she wasn't working today. I explained what was going on and he looked at me blankly. "We don't sell things on consignment," he said.

"Yes, you do," I told him.

"Look, I'm the owner of this store," he said firmly, "and I'm here to tell you we don't."

I felt like a stack of blocks that somebody had just kicked over. In a halting voice, I told the guy what Jade had told us.

"You've been ripped off," he said. "Jade must have sold your merchandise to another store, or maybe she scammed some other people like you and organized a craft sale in her house."

I felt so angry, so used. "That sucks!" I cried. "I'm calling the cops."

"Did you get a receipt when you left the merchandise with her?" he asked. I shook my head. "Then you don't have any evidence."

"But—"

"If I were you, I'd chalk this one up to experience," he said. "And thanks for telling me what's been going on. I hired Jade as temporary Christmas help. I was thinking of keeping her on, but now I won't. She's history."

Great, I thought, but what about me? I had to go back and tell Iris that all her stuff—including her favorite shirt—had disappeared, and we hadn't made one cent off them. Not only that, but her blossoming Melrose Avenue consignment business had just gone from promising to nonexistent.

I trudged back to our room, feeling like crap, knowing that I'd let Iris down. I'd told her that stores would want to buy her handmade clothes and jewelry. In fact, I'd practically promised her. But it wasn't true, at least not on Melrose Avenue. And now we were living in a slummy little room with no jobs and only $135 between us and homelessness.

I climbed the stairs with my stomach tied in knots. I knew Iris was going to be disappointed. I knew she was going to be scared. And I knew she was going to be pissed, both at Jade and at me. But I never expected to hear her say anything like what she said.

She waited until I'd told her the whole story. Then she got up from the bed where she'd been resting. "I'm calling Eddie," she said.

I felt my jaw drop. "Eddie?" I cried. "Are you nuts? Why would you want to talk to him?"

"I'm going to ask him to drive down here and pick me up," she said. "I'm going to ask him to take me back. And then I'm going to call your parents and tell them where you are."

"Don't you dare!" I shouted. "I'm not going back. Not ever!"

"Look, Sara, this was a fun little adventure we had, but it's over. I've got a kid to think about. It's time to get serious and figure out what I'm going to do."

"But it's all figured out," I insisted. "We're going to raise the baby together. We decided that when we left Laguna Verde."

"You decided it," she said. "I came along because I didn't have a better idea, and because I wanted to believe what you were telling me. But in my gut I always knew your whole Iris and Sara happily-ever-after story was just a fairy tale."

I felt sick inside. Iris was the only person I had left. The only one who cared about me. Just Iris and her baby. And now she was turning her back on me. "It's not a fairy tale," I said. "We can raise the baby ourselves. Okay, maybe it isn't as easy as I'd imagined. But listen, I've been thinking. If we move out of the city, maybe find some little town in the mountains—"

Iris cut me off with a shake of her head. "Your parents were right about a lot of things, Sara. I'm not ready to make a living selling clothes and jewelry. I need to go back to school. And this baby needs to live with a real mother and father, not a couple of teenagers."

"Why are you taking my parents' side all of a sudden?" I demanded. "Don't you realize they don't give a damn about you?"

"And who does give a damn about me?" she shot back. "You?" She laughed bitterly. "You're a nice kid, Sara, but you don't know much about the real world. I mean, this is just a game to you. When things get too rough, you can always run back to Mommy and Daddy. But me—this is my life." She looked around our grubby little room. "It's either Eddie or this. Those are my choices."

I felt scared, like I was hanging onto the edge of a cliff by my fingertips and Iris was stepping on my hands. "I know plenty about real life," I said. "I know you don't belong with a creep like Eddie. I know you're an artist. And I know I was meant to help raise that baby inside you. She belongs to us—to you and me."

"That's all you can think about, isn't it?" Iris asked. "Just you and your feelings. You know, I've got feelings, too, Sara. And opinions and ideas. I count."

I just couldn't believe Iris was talking to me like that. Why did she think I'd run away from home in the first place? Just for a laugh? No way. I'd done it for her. "Of course you count," I said. "I know that better than anyone."

"Then why do you keep pushing your opinions on me, trying to turn me into a carbon copy of you?" she demanded. "I don't want to eat veggie burgers, or listen to that lousy rap music we heard at the pro-choice concert. I don't even know why I went there. I think abortion is wrong."

I was so shocked, I could barely speak. "But you told me you considered having one," I whispered.

"No, I didn't. I said I didn't want to face the fact that I was pregnant, and by the time I did, it was too late to do anything except go through with it. But that doesn't mean I would have had an abortion. That's just what you wanted to hear."

My mind was spinning. "I didn't force you to go to that concert," I said, "or to come here, either. You were excited about selling your clothes on Melrose, and about raising the baby together. You can't tell me you weren't."

Iris took a breath. "Maybe you're right," she said. "I don't know anymore. All I know is I'm sick and exhausted and hungry and broke. I want to go somewhere where I can get a decent meal and sleep in a nice bed. And I want to find a family who will adopt my baby. I can't take care of it myself. I'm still learning how to take care of me."

Was she right? I didn't know. All I knew was that when I gazed into her eyes, I felt lost and alone, like I was slipping even farther off that cliff. I tried to say something that would convince her to stay, but all that came out was, "I thought we were friends."

"I thought so, too," she said. "But now I don't know. Maybe we were just using each other to get what we wanted out of this adoption. But what we ended up with was a screwed-up mess."

With that, she stood up, grabbed her purse, and walked out of the room. I knew she was going to call

Eddie and my parents, but I didn't try to stop her. What was the point? Her mind was made up.

I've been sitting here in the room ever since Iris left, trying to make sense of things. I can't believe I'm never going to see your face, Mystery Baby. Never going to hold you in my arms, or sing to you, or see your beautiful smile. And all the weeks of writing in this journal, what was the point? You're never going to read it. Never going to know about me, or my parents, or all the craziness and tears we went through just because of you.

I've got to take action, come up with some kind of plan, but my brain feels about as useful as that hunk-of-junk van we left Laguna Verde in. I don't trust myself anymore, not after everything that's happened. I mean, I thought I had the future all figured out. But nothing has worked out the way I expected it to. It's all been a disaster, a total mess.

Come on, Sara, think. I can't stay in this apartment building—not unless I want my parents to find me and drag me home. If they even want to. But where am I going to go? There's nothing left for me in Laguna Verde, and nothing left for me in L.A. Maybe I'll just—

I hear footsteps in the hall. Is it Iris? If only she was coming back to tell me she'd changed her mind. But why would she? I let her down, big time. It's no wonder she wants to go back to Eddie. At least he doesn't fill her head with fairy tales that can never come true.

It *is* Iris. I hear her key in the lock. Oh God, I can't face her. It's going to hurt too much to watch her pack her duffel bags and leave. I've got to get out of here. I've got to go somewhere until—

Christmas Day

It's over. I'm sitting in the lounge in the obstetrics ward, waiting to talk to the doctor. I should probably sleep, but I feel so nervous, so wired. So I'm scribbling this on the back of some scrap paper a nurse gave me. Maybe it will help me make some kind of sense of the last ten hours, if that's possible.

When Iris opened the door to our room, I knew right away that something was wrong. Her face was as white as chalk, and her eyelids were fluttering. As I jumped to my feet, she leaned heavily on the door frame and said in a hoarse whisper, "I started to call, but I think I fainted. I don't feel so good."

I put my arms around her and lugged her toward the bed.

"Sara?" she croaked. "Sara, where are you?"

"I'm right here," I said. "Everything's going to be okay. Just lie down a minute and—"

I felt something warm and wet against my leg. I

dragged Iris the rest of the way to the bed and put her down, then looked at my jeans. They were wet. I gasped and turned back to Iris. Her jeans were wet, too, and there was a blob of thick, mucusy fluid in the middle of the floor.

"Iris, what happened?" I cried, but her eyes were closed and her mouth was hanging open. My first thought was that she was dead. I felt panic rising in my throat. I leaned over her and pressed my head against her chest. Thank God! Her heart was beating.

I took a slow breath and tried to think. Then I remembered something I read in the birth book I took out of the library. It said that before a woman gives birth, the amniotic sac inside the uterus breaks, and the fluid that the fetus has been floating in gushes out. Usually it happens during labor, but sometimes it happens even earlier. When it does, it means the baby is on the way.

The panicky feeling leaped back into my throat. Iris was only eight months pregnant. She wasn't supposed to have her baby yet. But it was about to happen, whether Iris or I or that little person inside of her liked it or not.

I've never felt so alone and scared in my life. I had to do something. But what? For a moment, I was too confused to even think. Then, like a clock striking the hour, everything seemed to click into place and I knew what I had to do. I ran down to the lobby and shouted at the guy who was sitting in the little booth, "Call an ambulance. There's a woman about to give birth. She fainted and—"

He unlocked the door of the booth, opened it, and thrust the telephone receiver at me. "Do it yourself."

I dialed 911 and told the operator what had happened. I guess I must have been pretty hysterical because I couldn't remember our address or room number, but the guy in the booth told the operator and she promised to send an ambulance right away.

I ran back to the room. Iris hadn't moved. I grabbed one of her socks that was lying on the floor, wet it with cold water in the sink down the hall, and put it on her forehead. She groaned a little and then suddenly her jaw clenched and her eyelids squeezed together. Was she having a contraction? I wasn't really sure, but I grabbed her hand and held it tight.

We stayed that way for what seemed like forever. All sorts of random thoughts were bouncing through my brain. Was the ambulance ever coming? Maybe the operator had forgotten about us, or maybe she had simply decided Iris's problem wasn't very important. I tried to imagine what I would do if Iris had her baby right then, right there on the bed. But like a computer screen flashing the words DOES NOT COMPUTE, my brain wouldn't process the question.

Then finally I heard the whine of a siren, and a minute later two paramedics—one male, one female—ran into the room. "What happened?" the man asked as the woman listened to Iris's heart and took her blood pressure.

I gave him a rundown on the last half hour.

"Her blood pressure's way down," the woman broke in.

"Let's get her on an I.V., stat," the guy replied.

Together, he and the woman lowered Iris onto a portable stretcher. Then the woman stuck a needle in Iris's arm and hooked it up to a bottle of clear fluid.

"When's her due date?" the woman asked as they carried her downstairs. A small group of curiosity seekers had gathered on the sidewalk to watch.

"January 23," I said.

"You her sister?" the man asked.

"Her friend," I said, and then immediately felt like a hypocrite. Iris had said maybe we were just using each other to get what we wanted out of the adoption. Was that true? I didn't know, but I did know one thing. I wasn't thinking about myself now, or even about the baby. All I could focus on was Iris. I was so worried about her I was shaking. "Is she going to be all right?" I asked.

The paramedics had loaded Iris's stretcher into the ambulance. "If we get her blood pressure stabilized, she should be fine," the man said. "You'll have to wait until you get to the hospital to find out about the baby."

I didn't ask if I could come along. I just jumped in and knelt down beside Iris's stretcher. The female paramedic sat on the other side while the man climbed out and closed the door. A second later, we were careening down the street, siren wailing.

We hadn't gone more than a block before Iris's eyes fluttered open. "Wha—? Where—?" she muttered.

I reached out and took her pale hand. "Your water broke. We're on the way to the hospital."

"But it's too soon," she protested weakly.

I shook my head. "The kid just couldn't wait another second." Iris managed a weak smile. I smiled back. "It's going to be okay," I said, hoping it was true.

Iris's smile faded, and her eyes grew wide. "I think I'm having a contraction," she said. Then suddenly, she gritted her teeth, pressed her eyelids shut, and squeezed my hand tight. A strangled groan escaped from her lips.

I stared at her, feeling frightened and helpless. The look on her face reminded me of the woman we'd seen in the video at Iris's birthing class. And then suddenly I remembered those silly breathing exercises the instructor had made us do. Did they really help? I figured it was worth a try.

"Iris," I said in what I hoped was an authoritative voice. "Iris, look at me." She opened her eyes. "Breathe with me," I said.

She shook her head. "It hurts too much."

"Breathe with me," I said again, staring into her frightened eyes. "You can do it."

With my nose practically touching hers, I began hooing and heeing, just the way we'd done in the birthing class. I probably sounded like an idiot, but I didn't care. Iris joined in, hesitantly at first, then with more conviction. Our eyes were locked together, our fingers were intertwined. We were breathing together as if we were one person.

And then, gradually, the contraction ended and Iris's muscles relaxed. She released the death grip she had on my hand and closed her eyes.

"You did it," I said.

Iris smiled without opening her eyes. "Thanks," she whispered.

"Her blood pressure is back to normal," the paramedic said as the ambulance pulled up to the emergency room. She jumped up and opened the doors. The other paramedic appeared, and together they rolled Iris's stretcher toward the emergency room. I jogged beside them.

As we stepped into the emergency room, I froze. The place was exploding with people. They were sitting on the chairs, standing in the middle of the room, lying on the floor. Most of them were black or Latino or Asian, and all of them looked poor. There were women holding screaming babies, teenagers with slashed faces, elderly people with yellow skin and sunken eyes. One man was holding a dripping, bloody towel around his hand. A small pool of blood had collected on his shoes. Another was lying on the floor beside a puddle of urine.

"We want to go to a different hospital," I told the paramedics. I had to practically shout to be heard above the din. "How far is it to UCLA?"

"She got insurance?" the woman asked, indicating Iris.

I nodded. "She has some kind of state insurance. Medi-Cal, I think it's called."

"Then you haven't got a choice," the man said. "The other hospitals aren't going to accept her without private insurance—or cash."

I thought about my parents. If they were here, Iris never would have been brought to this dump in the first place. She'd be at the best hospital in L.A. no matter what it cost. I looked at Iris, lying helplessly on the stretcher, and thought back to the night Mom and Dad were reminiscing about my birth.

"Back then we thought love was all you needed to get by," Mom had said. And Dad had answered, "We learned differently pretty fast." I guess I was learning, too.

The paramedics lifted Iris off the stretcher and sat her down in an empty wheelchair. Then they walked away to talk to the nurse behind the reception desk. As they turned to leave, the nurse called me over.

"Your friend needs to sign these release forms," she said. "Then we'll take her into the labor room."

I stared at the papers. "Can't she do this later?" I pleaded. "She's about to have a baby."

The woman shrugged. "Sorry. Hospital policy."

God, I felt so helpless. Things were happening too fast, and with each passing second I felt more and more out of control. To make matters worse, Iris was having another contraction. I ran over and tried to help her through it. This one was much worse than the last, but we kept our eyes locked on each other and did our breathing until it passed.

Then we turned to the forms. While Iris scribbled her name on a variety of dotted lines, a nurse came around to take her blood pressure. She frowned as she watched the gauge. "Her pressure is too high."

"High?" I repeated. "The paramedics said it was too low."

"It might have been," she said, "but now it's going up. And high is serious." Without another word, she walked to the front desk.

Instantly, an orderly appeared and began wheeling Iris away. "Where are you taking her?" I cried, following him down a long corridor.

"The labor room," he said.

"What's wrong with me?" Iris asked in an alarmed voice.

"Don't ask me," the orderly said, shrugging as he pushed Iris's wheelchair through a set of double doors. "Ask the doctor."

The video we had seen in Iris's birthing class had

been shot in a private hospital room, with soothing paintings on the walls, comfortable furniture, and a big TV. But this labor room was more like a factory than a cozy birthing suite. It was huge—almost as big as our high school auditorium—with dirty beige walls and gray linoleum floors. Free-standing curtains had been set up at twenty-foot intervals, dividing the room into dozens of tiny cubicles. Inside each "room" was a woman in labor. The sounds of their grunts, pants, moans, and screams filled the air.

The orderly pushed Iris into an empty cubicle and left. "A contraction is coming," she said in a frightened voice. I grabbed her hand and we started to breathe. To our left we could hear a man arguing with a woman about who the father of her baby was. To the right, a woman was screeching like a wounded cat.

I looked into Iris's anxious eyes. What was wrong with her? I wondered. Where's the doctor? Is the baby going to be all right? I felt scared and powerless, but more than that, I felt ashamed. If it wasn't for me, I thought, we wouldn't be in this toilet. Iris would be in a cushy birthing room at the Laguna Verde Hospital, surrounded by doctors and nurses, being coached by people who actually knew what they were doing.

I thought about my mother and father again. I imagined them appearing at the entrance of Iris's cubicle, taking charge, making things happen. Part of me longed to call them up and beg them to come immediately, but another part of me resisted. It would mean humbling myself to them, admitting I'd failed, giving up. After all that I'd said and done, how could I do that?

Iris's contraction was over. As I reached out to wipe

the sweat from her forehead with my sleeve, a man in a white coat walked into the cubicle. He had nut-brown skin and a dark mustache. "How do you do," he said. "I'm Doctor Joshi."

"You're a doctor?" I asked. He looked young, hardly more than a teenager.

"I'm a first-year resident," he replied. He took Iris's blood pressure and tapped her knee with a reflex hammer. Then he leaned down to look her in the eye. "It appears you have preeclampsia." he said. "It's a condition that sometimes develops in pregnancy, characterized by hyperexcitability of the nervous system."

"Is it serious?" Iris asked anxiously. "I mean, will it hurt the baby?"

"It can, and it can have very serious consequences for you—seizures, possibly even stroke, or death. I'm going to give you an I.V. with some medicine that we hope will bring your blood pressure down. If that doesn't work, we'll discuss our next option."

I watched helplessly as a nurse helped Iris take off her jeans and climb up on a gurney. Within minutes Iris had a catheter between her legs, a fetal monitor stretched over her belly, and a new bottle attached to her I.V. line. She lay there like a deer strapped to a car fender, looking helpless and awkward and scared.

Please, I prayed to whatever god might be listening, please don't let her die.

Dr. Joshi took Iris's blood pressure again. I could tell by the look on his face that it was bad news. "The pressure has risen slightly. At this point, I feel we need to act aggressively, and that means getting the baby out as quickly as possible. We have two choices—

administering a drug to speed up the labor, or doing a C-section."

Iris looked like an animal caught in a trap. "I don't want to be cut open. Please."

Dr. Joshi nodded. "All right. We'll try the pitocin. But I must warn you, the contractions will intensify quickly." He smiled apologetically. "This isn't going to be fun."

The panicky feeling I had been holding in check for hours welled up inside me again. Had Iris made the right decision? Would she be able to handle the contractions? What if she had a seizure? What would happen to the baby? Should I tell her to have a C-section?

I watched as a nurse attached yet another bottle to her IV line. I knew Iris was looking to me to take care of her, to make everything all right. But who was going to take care of me? Suddenly, I didn't feel so cocky, so grown-up. Iris and her baby were depending on me, but who was I? Just a frightened little fifteen-year-old who didn't know what the hell I was doing.

Iris stretched out her hand to me. I stepped closer and took it. "You gotta help me get through this," she said in a desperate whisper. She pulled me closer and gazed deeply into my eyes. "Sara, I'm scared."

Looking into Iris's pleading eyes, my refusal to humble myself to my parents no longer seemed so important, so heroic. What it seemed like, in fact, was pure selfishness, pure stupidity. Iris needed all the friends she could get right now, including my parents. Especially my parents. If they would agree to come . . .

I decided to call them and find out.

Christmas Day, Continued

Thank God my parents were home. My father answered the phone. When I heard his voice, I clammed up. I just didn't know what to say.

"Hello?" he said. "Hello? Is anybody there?"

I thought about Iris and forced myself to speak. "Dad, it's me."

"Sara! Oh, thank God!" His voice was cracking with emotion. I felt surprised, guilty, happy. Maybe he did care about me. "Where are you?" he cried.

I gave him a rambling, halting explanation of what had been going on during the last couple of hours. Then I leaned my head against the phone booth and said the words I'd sworn I would never say. "Iris needs your help. I need your help. Please . . . can you and Mom come down here?"

"Good Lord, of course," he said. "We'll leave immediately."

"Thanks, Dad," I muttered.

"And Sara?" I waited. This is it, I thought. The part where he tells me what a difficult, troublesome, stupid child I am. But all he said was, "I love you." Then he hung up.

As I ran back to the labor room, tears of relief welled up in my eyes. Like a juggler with one too many balls in the air, I had been trying desperately for days now to hold everything together. The strain had been almost unbearable, but now at last it was over. I hated to give up, hated to admit I needed my parents' help. But at least I was no longer alone.

I entered the cubicle to find Iris in the midst of a killer contraction. She wasn't doing her breathing; she was screaming.

I ran up to her and shouted at her to look at me. Instead, she tried to push me away. But I knew the breathing could help—I'd seen it help—so I grabbed her wrists and leaned into her face. "Focus!" I ordered. "I want you to think of a safe, quiet place. Can you see it?"

Iris shook her head frantically.

"Some place where there's no pain. Just peace, just happiness. Can you find it, Iris?"

She hesitated, then nodded.

"Where is it?" I asked.

"Your backyard," she gasped, "underneath the big tree."

"Okay," I said, "let's climb the tree together. Can you see the ocean? Good. Now breathe."

We got through the contraction, and Iris lay back on the gurney with her arm draped over her eyes. After a minute she said, "Kind of pathetic, isn't it? Your back-yard is the safest, most peaceful place I've ever been."

I started to protest, but Iris cut me off.

"When you first started being nice to me, I couldn't figure out why. But I went along with it because I wanted to get a look at your world. I wanted to see what it was like to be one of the lucky ones." She opened her eyes and looked at me. "You don't know how good you have it, Sara. Your parents may be strict, they may enjoy throwing their weight around, they may be all sorts of lousy things you say they are. But they love you and protect you, and that's a hell of a lot."

I didn't answer. I was remembering something I wrote in this journal a long time ago—something about how hanging out with Iris was like being in a room with people who were smoking grass. Just being close to her gave me a contact high.

And it occurred to me that maybe Iris was right when she said we had used each other to get what we wanted out of the adoption. Maybe I was looking for an ally in my battle against my parents, and Iris fit the bill—an unwed mother, a high-school dropout, a runaway. She was everything my parents didn't want me to be. I admired her wild ways, her biker boyfriend, her independence; but at the same time, I felt sorry for her, too. So I used her, to help me rebel against my parents, and—just like my father had said—as my own personal charity case.

It was hard enough to get my head around that, but what shocked me even more was the realization that Iris had used me, too. I thought back to something she'd said the night she ate dinner at our house: "I want this kid to have the fancy crib, the toys, the big backyard. I want her to have two grown-up parents and a cool big sister. It's what I wish I had."

So maybe hanging out with me was a way for Iris to get close to the things she'd never had. And maybe I only thought she was siding with me against my parents. I mean, why should she want to rebel against them? Even if they did act condescendingly toward her sometimes, they still took care of her, gave her money, food, and best of all, a home for her baby. And in Iris's eyes, that was the next best thing to finding a home for herself.

"What you said back in the room was right," I told her. "I haven't been a real friend to you. If I had been, I wouldn't have talked you into running away from Laguna Verde."

Iris shook her head. "Look, you said it—nobody forced me to come. Nobody forced me to do anything. Anyway, you're saving my ass by helping me through these contractions. If that isn't friendship, I don't know what is." She grimaced. "Oh, God, here comes another one."

They were getting closer together now and much more intense. It was all I could do to keep Iris focused and breathing. Dr. Joshi came in to take another blood-pressure reading and to exchange Iris's external fetal monitor for a more accurate, internal one. Her pressure had stabilized, he said, but there was no guarantee it would stay that way. Plus, she was only five centimeters dilated. She had another five to go before the baby could fit through the birth canal.

"I'm going to increase your dose of pitocin and see if we can get things moving," he said. "But if you don't start progressing faster, we're going to have to go with the C-section."

"No," Iris said instantly. "I don't want to be cut open."

"But Iris," I began, "the baby—"

"The kid is going to be okay. We can do this— together. Please, Sara?"

What could I say? It was her body, her child. So we kept at it for another hour, panting and hugging, groaning and focusing, while Dr. Joshi and the nurses popped in and out, doing tests and looking worried. We were in the middle of the most intense contraction yet when my parents arrived. We didn't even notice them until it was over. Then my mother cleared her throat and said, "Sara, sweetheart—"

I turned, and for a brief instant I saw my parents the way a stranger would see them—not as my mother and father, not as my saviors or my role models or my enemies, but as two slightly plump, middle-aged, ordinary people. The impression only lasted a split second and then it was gone, but the memory has stayed with me. They seem somehow less mysterious now, less powerful and more human. They seem more real.

"Oh, my God!" Iris cried. "How did you know—?" She turned to me. "Sara, did you call them?"

That's when I realized I hadn't even told Iris about the phone call. Things had just been too hectic, too intense. I nodded, and Iris smiled. "You did the right thing," she said.

My parents threw their arms around me and hugged me hard, then they walked over to Iris and hugged her, too. I figured a lecture about how Iris and I had screwed up royally would come next, but no. Dad simply strode out of the cubicle, collared the nearest orderly, and demanded in his most authoritative voice to see the doctor.

We were waiting for Dr. Joshi when Iris had her next contraction. Mom took over, talking her through it, helping her breathe. I've never seen my mother so gentle and caring, yet so confident and in control at the same time. Inside, she had to be freaking, but she didn't show it. Iris picked up the vibe and stayed on top of the pain. She was more relaxed, more focused than I'd seen her since we arrived at the hospital.

Meanwhile, Dr. Joshi came in and my father started to grill him about Iris's condition. At one point I heard him ask my father what his relationship was to the patient. I expected him to say something about the adoption, but he didn't. All he said was, "She's a close friend of my daughter. We're a bit like an aunt and uncle to her."

Dr. Joshi nodded and took Iris's blood pressure again. Then he tapped her knee with his reflex hammer. Her leg jumped, then trembled. The doctor turned to us, his jaw set. "The pressure is going up again and her reflexes are much too active. We're doing a C-section immediately."

Iris pushed herself up on one arm. "Just check my dilation one more time. I think that last contraction made a difference. Maybe the baby's about to be born."

Dr. Joshi hesitated. Then he put his hand under the sheet that covered Iris. A look of surprise came over his face. "You're nine centimeters and almost completely effaced. There's a chance you could have the baby vaginally. But I don't recommend it. It's just too dangerous."

"I can do it," Iris insisted. She turned to Mom and Dad. "Tell him. They don't need to cut me open."

Mom and Dad exchanged a glance, then Mom said, "Give us just a moment, Dr. Joshi. We need to talk to Iris." The doctor nodded and left the cubicle. My parents turned to Iris. Mom took her hand. "What's wrong?" she asked gently.

Iris took a ragged breath. "My big sister died on an operating table. They said one of the valves in her heart was leaking, but when they cut her open, she died."

I was puzzled. Hadn't Iris told us she was the oldest child in her family? Mom and Dad must have been thinking the same thing, but all Dad said was, "That must have been an awful blow to you."

"She was more like a mother to me than my own mother," Iris said, the words catching in her throat. "After she died, I became the oldest. The other kids turned to me to hold things together." She wiped her eyes with the back of her hand and added bitterly, "I don't trust doctors. They always want to get inside you and start cutting. Half the time it just makes things worse."

Now I understood, and my parents did, too. "You're scared," Mom said. "Anyone would be. But you can't risk having a seizure or a stroke. It's not just the baby we're thinking about—we gave up any claim we had on your child when we let you run out our front door— it's you."

"Iris, listen to me," my father said. "Sara accused us of caring more about your baby than we do about you.

I realize now that she wasn't entirely wrong. We wanted to be parents so much, we let ourselves forget one essential, undeniable fact—unless you decide otherwise, that child inside you belongs to you and only you."

"Your baby needs you," Mom told Iris. "Please, let Dr. Joshi do the C-section. Don't do it for us, or for the doctor, or even for yourself. Do it for your child."

Iris didn't answer. Tears were streaming down her cheeks. Then finally, she turned to me. "Sara," she said in a small, wavering voice, "go get Dr. Joshi. He needs to get my baby out now."

After that, things happened fast. Before I could even tell Iris good-bye, an orderly was wheeling her out of the cubicle and off to the delivery room. My father told the nurse we wanted to go in with Iris, but she said it wasn't allowed. But Dad wasn't about to take no for an answer. He collared another nurse and got directions to the changing room, but when we finally found it (after taking three different wrong turns), we discovered they had run out of scrubs (those green pajama-like outfits they make you wear). And by the time we found an orderly and he located more scrubs and we got changed and washed and found the delivery room, the operation was already in progress, and no one could get in anyway.

The whole situation was so absurd, like the Marx Brothers meet *General Hospital*, that we would have laughed if we hadn't been so hysterical and frantic and worried to death. So here we are, sitting in the obstetrics lounge with our hearts in our throats, waiting to hear if Iris and the baby are all right. I'm trying to keep busy by writing this, Mom is obsessively running her hand over her dress, trying to take out the imaginary wrinkles, and Dad is grabbing every hospital employee who wanders by the room and demanding they give him some information.

Oh, thank God, at last. Here comes Dr. Joshi!

December 26

Dear Mystery Baby,

Joy to the world! You're alive and well, Little One. Kind of small—only five pounds, eight ounces—and you had to spend your first day on Earth in an incubator with a tube up your nose, but one hundred percent okay. And Iris is okay, too. Just fine, in fact, considering they knocked her out (Dr. Joshi said they needed to use general anesthesia to make sure she didn't have a seizure during the procedure), sliced open her belly, ripped out a baby, and then stitched her back up again.

You were born on Christmas day—talk about a great present!—at exactly 9:52 p.m. And guess what? You're a boy, which just goes to show you I've been wrong about practically everything concerning this adoption. But I was right about one thing. I loved you the instant I laid eyes on you. I adore the shape of your head (all round and perfect because you didn't have to wiggle your way through a birth canal), your tiny fingers and toes, your wide, wondering eyes, and the reddish-brown peach fuzz on the top of your head. I mean, we're talking serious crush here. When I reached my hand into the incubator and you grabbed my little finger, I practically swooned with delight.

Okay, so I'm a pushover. But if you promise to be good and not cry (yeah, right—by the time you read this you'll be big enough to lift me over your head) I'll tell you what happened next.

After Dr. Joshi told us the C-section had been a success, my parents and I screamed and hugged each other and jumped up and down. Then we stopped, backed up, and just stood there looking at each other. I mean, talk about a big letdown. Mom, Dad, and I had spent the last three months of our lives in constant turmoil—arguing, crying, attacking each other—all in an effort to figure out what this baby was going to mean to our family. Only now it was over and the baby wasn't ours. The adoption wasn't going to happen. We were back at square one, only with a lot more unresolved anger, sorrow, and guilt than we'd started with.

Dr. Joshi said it would be best if we waited until tomorrow to visit with Iris, and it didn't seem right to see her baby before she did, so there was nothing to do except leave the hospital. It was too far to go home, and my parents were too exhausted to drive anyway, so they rented a suite in a hotel in downtown L.A. After those filthy rooms Iris and I had been living in, the suite seemed like a palace—soft beds, clean sheets, plush carpets, and our very own bathroom.

I flopped down on the sofa and stared into space. I was exhausted, but too hyper to sleep. Mom sat down next to me and asked, "Sara, are you all right?"

I nodded. Then it occurred to me that I hadn't eaten anything in about twelve hours. "I'm starving," I said.

So we ordered room service—a feast of steak sandwiches, (grilled cheese for me), french fries, chocolate cake, and sodas. After I'd gorged myself, my father asked, "What have you been eating the last couple of days? Where have you been staying?"

"We called the police, talked to all your friends," my mother said, too upset to wait for my answer. "We hired a private detective the day before you called us. Oh, Sara—"

"Let her talk, Jeanette," Dad interrupted, which surprised me. Could it be that he really wanted to hear what I had to say? "Go on," he urged. "Tell us what happened."

I started slowly and pretty soon I couldn't stop. I just stared at my knees and talked—about calling Marc, meeting Cody in The Spot, the van breaking down, hitchhiking, Union Station, Melrose Avenue, the Edgemont Arms, the Dog House, the ambulance, everything. When it was over, I realized I was crying. I looked up at my parents, not knowing what to expect from them, not even sure what I wanted.

What I got was everything. Mom and Dad didn't say a word. They simply put their arms around me and held me. That's when I really started sobbing. I don't know how long we sat like that, just holding each other. It seemed like forever. But finally I just couldn't cry anymore. I looked up through my wet eyelashes, my nose running, my throat ragged, my breath coming in trembling sighs—and started to laugh.

"What?" my father said, half-amused, half-irritated.

"I don't know," I giggled. "I guess I just realized something. You really do love me, don't you?"

Now it was my father who was laughing. "Sara, you are the most infuriating child in the entire universe!" Then he grew serious and looked me in the eye. "You scared us more than you'll ever know. Promise me you'll never do anything like that again."

Mom nodded. "No matter how bad things get, we can always find a solution," she said. "You don't have to run away."

"I promise," I said. And then I told them all the stuff I'd been thinking about—how maybe I had viewed Iris as some sort of symbol of danger, rebellion, and freedom, and how I'd used her and the whole adoption thing to assert my independence from them.

They listened, then Mom nodded. "I think I can understand that. On the surface, it felt like we were fighting about Iris and her rights, but maybe what we were really arguing about was who was in control—of the adoption and of this family."

Dad laughed sadly. "Only we forgot that Iris was in control the whole time—of the adoption, anyway. It was her body, her baby. If our battles helped her figure that out, then I suppose they weren't all bad."

"I think they helped me figure out a few things," Mom said. "I thought I wanted another baby, but if it's going to make Sara feel left out or unloved or second-best, then it just isn't worth it to me." She took my hand. "Nothing is worth that."

"Stop being so nice to me," I protested. "I don't deserve it. Don't you realize I completely screwed up? I told Iris we could raise her baby together, I convinced her to run away with me, I said she could make a living as an artist. Yeah, right, Sara. Thanks to me, she ended up so sick and hungry and exhausted that she went into labor a month too early. If she had died, it would have been totally my fault."

My father looked at me grimly. "You made plenty of mistakes," he agreed. "Serious ones. And don't think we aren't going to dole out some pretty serious punishments."

I opened my mouth to complain, but then I shut it again. I had just done my best to convince my parents I'd behaved like a selfish ass. How obnoxious would it be to start whining because my convincing had worked? No, for once I was going to keep my mouth shut and let my parents rake me over the coals.

Instead, they did just the opposite. "Don't beat yourself up over what happened, Sara," my father continued. "You made a mess of things all right, but when everything came crashing down around you, you really came through. You got Iris to the hospital, you helped her through her labor. And in the end, you had the good sense to call us and ask for help."

"We were watching you when you didn't know we were there," Mom pointed out. "We saw how you took charge and helped Iris through her contraction." She smiled and shook her head. "I didn't even think you'd been paying attention during the birthing class. I guess sometimes I underestimate you."

I shrugged, feeling embarrassed and pleased. No one said anything for a minute. Then Mom yawned and stretched. "I think we've had enough excitement for one day," she said. "What do you say we all go to bed?"

Mom and Dad had thrown together pajamas and a few toiletries before they'd left, so I was able to brush my teeth with my own toothbrush and slip into my favorite flannel nightgown. I lay there in the pullout bed, listening to the familiar sounds of my parents getting ready for bed in the other room. I felt very happy and very, very sad. We were a family again, but it hadn't happened without casualties.

I thought about Iris, lying in her hospital bed. Tomorrow morning we would be saying good-bye to her, and to her new baby. After that, we would never see each other again. I felt a pang of loneliness in my chest, and I realized that despite all the confused ulterior motives that had complicated our relationship, we really had been friends.

But that was all over now. I was losing my little almost-sibling and my big sister/fellow-rebel/best friend. And I knew I was always going to miss them.

The next morning, we went to the hospital to visit Iris. They had put her in a room with four other women. When we arrived, she was sitting up in bed, listlessly leafing through a magazine.

I stepped up to her bed, feeling a little shy and awkward. After everything we'd been through, it was hard to know how to act toward each other. I guess my parents felt the same way, because my father cleared his throat and said in his bright, phony restaurant voice, "How's the new mother?"

Iris glanced at me and I rolled my eyes. She laughed—one of her husky, throaty laughs—and everything seemed to fall into place again. It was Iris and me against my parents—only with a difference. In the past, my father's pseudo-cheery voice had always filled me with disgust; today, I felt slightly annoyed, but mostly sympathetic. I knew he was trying to make the best of an uncomfortable situation.

"I'm okay, I guess," Iris said. "Tired. And it really hurts." She motioned toward her stomach and groin. "Down there."

"You're going to have to take it easy for a while," Mom said. "I'm sure Dr. Joshi told you that."

My instinctive reaction was to say, "Why don't you move in with us for a few weeks? We can take care of the baby while you rest." But I kept my mouth shut. I mean, I would have loved to have Iris stay with us. But I knew it would be awkward for my parents, and probably for Iris as well. So for once, I decided to just go with the flow and not try to manipulate the world into doing my bidding. It was an odd feeling, but at the same time, kind of liberating.

As it turned out, my parents had their own solution. "We'd like to continue helping you with your rent and food for a couple of months," my father said. "Just until you get back on your feet and find a job."

Iris looked embarrassed and grateful and proud. I was sure she was going to refuse my father's offer, but before she could open her mouth, my mother purposely changed the subject. "Have you held the baby yet?" she asked, with a smile.

Iris stared down at her hands and shook her head.

Mom looked puzzled. "Is something wrong? I mean, Dr. Joshi told us the baby would probably be out of the incubator by today. I thought you'd want to start feeding him."

Iris fingered her beaded leather bracelet. "I told the nurses not to bring him to me," she muttered.

"But why not?" I blurted out.

"If I hold him, I might not be able to give him up. And I know I have to."

"You mean, you're not going to keep him?" my mother cried. She looked shocked and concerned . . . and maybe a tiny bit hopeful.

"I can't give that kid the things I want him to have," she answered. "I always knew that, and the last few days just proved it."

"But—but—" my father stammered, "have you found a couple to adopt him?"

Iris shook her head. "Dr. Joshi said I should talk to one of the hospital social workers. She's coming to see me this afternoon."

A dozen different emotions were playing across my parents' faces. I knew how they were feeling because I felt the same way. I still wanted to be your big sister, Little Bro, but was it too late? Would Iris allow us to adopt you? And if she did, what would happen to the relationship between my parents and me? We had just started to make the first fledgling attempts to rebuild the mess that had once been our family. But we still had a long way to go. Would adopting Iris's baby knock us apart again? I didn't have the answer, but I was willing to take that chance.

Mom looked at Dad, then they both looked at me. I turned to Iris. "Could we—?" I stammered. "I mean, would you—?" I laughed foolishly and started again. "What I mean is, I know we aren't the perfect, all-American family we tried to pretend we were, but we really do care about you, Iris, and . . . well . . . if you let us raise your baby, we can promise him a nice backyard, and about half a million fancy toys, and a family who really, truly loves him."

Iris looked baffled. She turned to my parents. "You mean, you still want to adopt my baby?"

"I never stopped wanting it," Mom said. "I just didn't want to destroy the family I already had."

"And things are different now?" Iris asked tentatively.

"Yes," I said with conviction. I couldn't put it into words exactly, and I knew we still had a lot of unresolved issues hanging over our heads, but I felt deep down in the pit of my stomach that our family was strong and solid enough to welcome a new member.

"If you're sure . . ." Iris paused and looked at my Mom and Dad. "Then I'd like you to be the parents of my son. And, Sara," she added, smiling at me, "I want you to be his sister."

February 2

DEAR SKYLER,

I read over these letters the week after you came home from the hospital. I knew then that there were a few more things I wanted to get down on paper for you to read someday, but for some reason I just never managed to get around to it. And then today, something happened that made me understand why I hadn't done it. It's because the story of your adoption wasn't over yet, at least not for me. Only now it is, and Little Bro, guess what? It's a happy ending. Or maybe I should call it a happy beginning. Hmm, I'll let you be the judge.

We stayed with Iris until she told us she needed to rest, then we went down to the Neonatal ICU to see you for the first time. The nurses took you out of your incubator a couple of hours later, and we fed you your first bottle; you haven't stopped eating since. Are you planning to be a sumo wrestler or something, kid? I'm going to have to get a job just so we can afford to buy your formula!

Iris was discharged from the hospital two days later, the same day you were. I told Mom and Dad that I thought we should all drive back to Laguna Verde together. They looked a little tweaked—I think they assumed I no longer believed that birthmothers and adoptive families should have a personal relationship with each other. But I do. I mean, I know now that the relationship Iris and I had went too far, but I still believe my parents didn't go far enough. I think they realize that now, too. They didn't say it in so many words, but while Iris was still in the hospital, Mom told her she was sorry they'd pressured her into signing those papers in the lawyer's office.

"We thought if we put everything down in black and white, nothing could go wrong," she said. "But adoption isn't the same as a real-estate transaction. It involves real people with real emotions. You have to remain open, you have to trust that things will work out for the best. I don't think we understood that then."

Anyway, I guess Mom and Dad decided to listen to me for once, because we did drive Iris back to Laguna Verde with us. We asked her what her plans were, but she refused to tell us. I just hoped she wasn't planning to go back to Eddie. When we got to L.V. she asked us to drop her off at the bus station, and she promised to contact us once she got settled.

Outside the station, Dad wrote a check and slipped it into her pocket. She started to protest, then changed her mind, shrugged, and said, "Thanks." Then she paused, shuffled her feet, and asked if she could hold you one time.

Mom and Dad looked pretty freaked, but they got a grip on themselves and said, "Of course, Iris."

Your birthmother took you in her arms and gazed lovingly into your eyes. She stayed like that for about a minute. Then she said, "Have a nice life, kid," and handed you back to Mom.

She turned to go. Then she stopped and said, "I almost forgot." She reached into her duffel bag (Mom and Dad had retrieved her stuff from the room where we'd been staying) and handed me something. It was an infant-sized beaded leather bracelet, just like the one she wears. Just like the one she'd made for me.

I laughed, but there were tears in my eyes. "Thanks," I said, giving her a hug. "He's going to be the best-dressed baby in all of Laguna Verde."

Iris smiled. Mom and Dad each gave her a hug. Then she picked up her duffel bags and walked into the bus station.

Later that week, Dad called the gas station where we'd left Iris's van. He paid for the repairs with his credit card and arranged to have the mechanic drive it back to our house. It's here if Iris ever wants it. If not, Dad says I can have it next year when I get my license.

The punishment my parents cooked up wasn't at all what I expected. Instead of grounding me until my eighteenth birthday or forcing me to eat raw meat, they sent me to therapy. I go Mondays by myself and we go on Fridays as a family. It's been intense, sometimes really painful, but mostly good. I think I'm starting to understand my parents, and even like them once in a while. It's a unique, unexpected feeling.

When I returned to school, I told Lauren and Forest everything that had happened. I guess they told a few other people who told some other people because pretty soon everyone knew I was the girl who had run off with the birthmother of my adopted baby brother. The school's reaction was pretty much the same as when Marc staged the BLT protest—some people thought I was a jerk, a few were impressed, most people couldn't have cared less. But Ms. Steiner used the whole thing to start a class discussion about adoption rights.

One person who did seem impressed was Marc. Suddenly, he was interested in me again. He made a big deal out of buying me lunch one day—a cheese sandwich, which the school has now agreed to offer as its daily vegetarian entree—and telling me about the protest demonstration he staged on the day before Christmas vacation, the day after Iris and I ran away. Apparently, Noah, Lauren, Forest, and he really did wear butcher's smocks splattered with cow's blood. Jake Halsey and his buddies responded by flinging milk cartons at them, so Marc took out a baggy full of cow's blood and threw it at Jake. That led to a fist fight, and when it was all over, Marc and Jake were both suspended.

A couple of months ago, I probably would have been hanging on Marc's every word, but I guess things have changed. I still admire his talent as a rabble-rouser, but I know now that every event Marc is involved in is really just a showcase for Marc and his amazing ego. Forget politics. This guy's real calling is show business. Anyway, I'm still working on the Social Service Committee, but that's as far as my relationship with Marc goes. Last week he asked me if I wanted to go to a

PETA meeting with him down in L.A. I said thanks but no thanks.

The one person I hadn't talked to since I'd come back from L.A. was Cody. I saw him in the halls practically every day, but he made a point of never looking at me. Sometimes I thought about going up and talking to him, but what would I say? Anyway, I figured he'd probably just look down his nose at me and say, "See? I told you two teenagers couldn't raise a baby by themselves." Well, thank you very much, but I know that already. I don't need to have my nose rubbed in it by someone whose opinion really matters to me.

Meanwhile, there's you to take care of, Little Bro. You don't have colic, thank God, so we don't have to run the vacuum cleaner to get you to zone out, but you still have quite a set of lungs on you. When you wake up for your one A.M. feeding—that one is my responsibility—believe me, I know it.

Being a big sister is pretty cool, although I have to admit that watching Mom and Dad heap endless attention on you sometimes makes me feel a little left out. In other ways, though, you've made me feel more a part of this family than ever before. I'm sharing the responsibility of raising you, and Mom and Dad really are treating me more like an individual and an adult. And what's weird is that I'm starting to understand them better, especially their extremely infuriating (when it's directed at me) overprotectiveness. Because I feel the same way about you, Skyler.

Sometimes I wish you could just stay an infant forever so you wouldn't have to skin your knee, or fall in love with the wrong person, or wonder why your birthmother gave you away. But I know you can't. So

I'm just going to have to do my best to pick you up when you fall, and comfort you when you cry, and maybe sometimes even refuse to let you do something and then hit you with that obnoxious line, "Because I'm older than you and I said so, that's why."

Speaking of your birthmother, we got a letter from her last week. She moved back to Indio. She hasn't contacted her parents, but she's gotten in touch with her brothers and sisters. She's living on her own, working part-time as a maid in a hotel and going to junior college. Oh, and here's the coolest part—she's selling her handmade clothes and jewelry at a weekly street fair in Palm Springs. She sends her love, especially to you, Little One. I'm going to ask Mom and Dad to invite her to visit us over Easter vacation, but who knows if she'll come. She sounds pretty busy.

Now here's the last thing I want to tell you, Sky. Today the lawyer called to tell us that Eddie had signed the consent papers. Apparently, he had refused for a while—not because he wanted you to live with him, but because he wanted to throw his weight around and punish Iris for leaving him in the only way he knew how—but he finally got tired of the lawyer's persistent phone calls and gave in. I hope someday he gets his act together and does something to show you he cares. In the meantime, your adoptive dad will be here to give you all the love you can handle.

To celebrate Eddie's signing the consent, I decided to take you for a walk by the ocean. I bundled you up, strapped you into your stroller (the one with the fat tires for off-road adventures), and headed for Stony Beach. The waves were big and booming and there were surfers everywhere. I stopped and watched as one of them blasted down a wall of water, got tubed, then rocketed off the lip. "You gonna do that someday, Skyler?" I asked.

But you weren't even looking. Instead, you were gazing with wonder at the sky. You've been doing that ever since the first day we took you out of the hospital. That's why we decided to name you Skyler—but of course by the time you read this, you'll have heard that story so many times you'll want to barf.

Anyway, there we were at the edge of the water, gazing at the waves and the clouds respectively, when all of sudden this dude in a full winter wetsuit came surfing right at us. I guess he had started on an outside wave and worked it all the way to the inside. Now the wave was about to break on the shore and he was still riding.

"Watch out!" I shouted as he came at us. I grabbed your stroller and started to pull it out of the way, but at the last second he jumped off his board, yanked the leash, and scooped it up. Then he strolled out of the water.

"Hey, what's the matter with you?" I shouted. "Don't you realize you almost plowed right into us?"

He pulled off his wetsuit hood and my jaw dropped. It was Cody. He froze and looked at me, then at you, then back at me again.

"I'm sorry," he said in a subdued voice. "I didn't see you. The sun was in my eyes."

He started to walk away and I started to let him. Then I realized that I didn't want him to go, and that if I didn't stop him, I was going to regret it for a long, long time. So I took a deep breath and said, "This is my little brother, Skyler. My adopted brother."

Cody kneeled down in front of you and grinned. "Hi, little dude," he said. You stared at him and cooed.

"He must like you," I said. "That's the first time he's stopped looking at the sky all morning."

"He likes the wide blue yonder, huh?"

"Likes? He's a cloud junkie. My father thinks he's going to be a meteorologist or an astronomer."

"Or a space cadet like his big sister," Cody cracked.

"Hey," I said, my temper flaring like a beach bonfire. "What's that supposed to—?"

"I'm sorry," he said, standing up and turning to face me. "It was a lame joke." He paused. "Listen, Lauren told me what happened in L.A. I can't say I'm sorry, but . . . well, I know it must have been rough. I'm just glad everything turned out all right." He looked at me like he was trying to read my mind. "It did turn out all right, didn't it, Sara?"

Gazing into his blue eyes, I felt the way you must feel, Little Bro, when you're looking up at the sky. I was enraptured, I was mesmerized. I think I was falling in love. "It turned out better than all right. I've got a new brother, and Iris has a new life."

Cody knelt down and grinned at you again. "I love babies. They're like a whole new beginning."

Wow, what an opening. How could I not take advantage of it? I mean, I knew that what I was about to say was corny, but what the heck. I figured if Cody burst out laughing I could always throw myself into the ocean. "Do . . . do you think we could have a new beginning, too?" I asked.

Cody did laugh, but not in a mean way. "Maybe," he said. "If you promise you're not planning to use me as a case study for your PhD dissertation on adopted children."

Now it was my turn to laugh. "I swear it," I said, raising my right hand. "But do you think maybe I can still ask you some questions once in a while?" I motioned to you, sitting in your stroller. You had begun waving your arms and legs and whimpering. "I might need some advice along the way. And Skyler's going to need a role model who can show him it's okay to be adopted. A role model like you."

Cody unbuckled your seat belt and picked you up. Despite the fact that he was wearing a cold, dripping wetsuit, and that it was touching your soft, little cheek, you stopped fussing immediately. "No problem," Cody said, smiling down at you. "I'm available."

What is it about this guy that makes me feel like a dripping pool of sap? I don't know, but I couldn't help myself. I waited until he looked over at me. Then I smiled adoringly like some heroine in a romance novel, and purred, "Me, too."

Cody laughed, pretended he was about to retch, and then kissed me. Then we walked up the beach to get his towel—Cody, me, and you, the former Mystery Baby, now known to the world as Skyler Boone Dewherst. My little brother.

Thought-Provoking Novels
from Today's Headlines

HOMETOWN
by Marsha Qualey 72921-0/$3.99 US/$4.99 Can
Border Baker isn't happy about moving to his father's rural Minnesota hometown, where they haven't forgotten that Border's father fled to Canada rather than serve in Vietnam. Now, as a new generation is bound for the Persian Gulf, the town wonders about the son of a draft dodger.

NOTHING BUT THE TRUTH
by Avi 71907-X/$4.50 US /$5.99 Can
Philip was just humming along with *The Star Spangled Banner*, played each day in his homeroom. How could this minor incident turn into a major national scandal?

TWELVE DAYS IN AUGUST
by Liza Ketchum Murrow 72353-0/$3.99 US/$4.99 Can
Sixteen-year-old Todd is instantly attracted to Rita Beckman, newly arrived in Todd's town from Los Angeles. But when Todd's soccer teammate Randy starts spreading the rumor that Rita's twin brother Alex is gay, Todd isn't sure he has the courage to stick up for Alex.

THE HATE CRIME
by Phyllis Karas 78214-6/$3.99 US/$4.99 Can
Zack's dad is the district attorney, so Zack hears about all kinds of terrible crimes. The latest case is about graffiti defacing the local temple. But it's only when Zack tries to get to the bottom of this senseless act that he fully understands the terror these vicious scrawls evoke.